THE STONE COIN

SASKIA WOODHILL

A catalogue record of this book is available from the National Library of New Zealand

Lightpool Publishing

www.lightpoolpublishing.com

1

It was a cool, clear Saturday afternoon, the kind of day you sometimes get after two days of rain, when the air seems more transparent than usual and everything looks crisp and clear. Mary was crossing the street from the bus stop to the French Bistro when her phone signalled a message. It was from Andrea and said she'd be fifteen minutes late or possibly more, she had to call her mother back and it might take time - and Mary knew just how true that was. She had long been familiar with Mrs Franklin's inability to end a conversation without going over everything at least twice.

Andrea had been Mary's protector from her second year at school. Until then her dad had dropped her at the school gate, but now she could walk, like the other children. It was just two blocks from their house, but every day, Andrea, who was three years older, waited for her at the Lintott's gate and they walked together to and from school. If Andrea was sick and not going to school her mother would call Mary's house and her dad or one of her brothers would take her.

Not until she was adult had Mary wondered who set this arrangement up and asked her father to explain it. 'Oh, I did,' he said quite casually. 'I knew the Franklins long before you were born, not like close friends, but they're good people. And I knew they had a girl at your school, a bit older than you, and their kids had to walk past our place on the way to school. So I asked if they'd be in on this, so you didn't have to be taken to school by your father every day - in case you felt it was a bit over the top.'

The French Bistro was one of Mary's favourite haunts, the one she always suggested when someone asked where they should meet. She stopped just inside the door and looked around and thought once again how weird and eclectic the place was, a mixture of styles and eras that had evolved over decades. Her father had told her he used to go there many years ago with his first wife, and over the decades since, various managers had added their own touch. The framed tourism posters of French beauty spots looked as if they had been there from the very start, slightly yellowed, and someone had added modern uplighters for the walls and draped lines of bud lights over the bar, but what Mary thought of as the cosy corner had apparently been there from when the place first opened. And today that corner was still available, so she went to the bar and asked for a "reserved" sign and put it on the round table in the alcove, which she knew would be taken very soon if she left it.

Leaving her jacket on the curved banquette she headed

for the restroom, where she went through her normal routine, checked the empty stalls for the one that looked as if it hadn't been used since it was last cleaned and then looked closely into the corners. The article she had read a few weeks ago about a man who was in court on a charge of installing tiny cameras in women's toilets had alerted her to something she'd never heard about before, so now she always had a good look. She remained in front of the wash basin for a minute after washing her hands and studied herself in the mirror. Today was the first time she had worn her new top, bought on an impulse some weeks ago, and not taken out of the drawer since. She had never worn that shade of nearly fluorescent lime green before and had regretted the purchase as soon as she got home, but today she finally put it on. It was ok, she decided, a bit more dramatic than what she normally wore, and it would draw attention to her, but perhaps she would get used to it. That strong, clear colour together with her thick, black hair curling down to her shoulders would make her stand out, but she knew Andrea would comment positively and say it was high time she used her looks to best advantage instead of trying to look inconspicuous.

When she exited the little passage from the restrooms, the bar had become crowded, and as she made to thread her way through, a man stepped sideways just as she went to go around him, and they collided quite hard.

'God, I'm sorry!' He swung around to face her. 'Are you hurt? I should have been more careful.'

'Not at all! And it was m-my own fault. I should have walked along the wall instead of through this l-lot.'

'They just appeared out of nowhere.' The very good looking man shook his head and grinned. 'I'd just got here and suddenly I was hemmed into this corner by a dozen guys, and they just kept moving further in as if they were herding me. Hey, I think I've seen you somewhere before. Have we met?'

She studied his face to work out if he was sincere, and that this was not just an overused pick-up line. 'I d-don't think so, but I come here often, so you m-might have seen me.'

'I'm Greg,' he said. 'Are you with someone? Can I buy you a drink to compensate for nearly knocking you over?'

She returned his smile - it was nearly impossible not to. 'I'm waiting for a f-friend who's going to be a bit l-late, so no thanks. I'll wait and order when she arrives.'

Five minutes later they were still talking, and Mary noted that Greg gave out none of the little signals some did when they first entered into conversation with her. Some people found her stammer disturbing, and she always knew when this happened. But there was something else going on, nothing to do with her stammer, just a little background noise in her mind telling her something was slightly off, and though she couldn't make up her mind why she got this impression, she decided to keep things cool. This phenomenon had occurred two or three times in the past and turned out to be an advance warning that someone was lying or perhaps not being upfront about who they were. She had no idea if it was something others experienced too, but with the inherent caution that was part of her nature she decided to take things carefully with this handsome guy.

'You know what Saturn is, right?' he said suddenly, a comment that came right out of the blue, unconnected to what they had just talked about.

She said casually, 'It's a gas giant, a p-planet without a solid s-surface? What about it?'

He gave her that stunning smile again, a mixture of a little boy playing a prank and a very attractive, adult male. 'Wow! You're very surprising, you really are, very quick. So following on from your knowledge about gas planets, do you also know what a Saturnalia is?'

He was clearly the kind of man who thought pretty girls were stupid or silly, she decided and smiled inside, so definitely a man to keep ay arm's length. She allowed herself to sound bored. 'Is this a quiz? Saturnalia was an ancient Roman f-feast, a bit l-like our Christmas, I think. What about it?'

'My friends are organising one this year, not now, in a couple of months. Maybe you'd like to come.'

She nearly said, 'Not including a Roman orgy, I hope?' but introducing a sexual reference would definitely be a mistake with this man, who didn't need his chatting-up technique bolstered by any suggestive comments from her. He's too sexy for his own good, she told herself, I bet woman literally fall into his lap, so don't sound intrigued. The more she listened to him the more certain she felt that there was something else going on, she could still sense that little background noise in her mind, and she needed to figure it out before she committed herself to anything. But despite her initial impression, it might be the fact that she stammered, which she always did apart from with her immediate family – some people found it disturbing.

'I'm n-not sure,' she said slowly, as if she was considering his invitation. 'There's a lot going on in m-my family in the next few weeks, so p-probably no, but thanks for asking.'

If he was surprised by her lack of enthusiasm he hid it well. 'I hope you'll change your mind. They did it a couple of years ago as a different way of having an early Christmas party, but I was overseas at the time. The pictures I saw on social media looked great - people dressed in togas and drinking red wine out of silver goblets, and someone playing a harp in a corner, one of those small ones you hold on your knee.'

Just then Mary spotted Andrea coming in and used it as an excuse to avoid giving him a definite answer. 'Sorry, there's my f-friend. I must go and t-tell her I'm still here. She's got something serious she wants to t-talk about, so I can't keep her wondering where I've got to. Nice to m-meet you.'

He was clearly taken aback by her lack of overt interest. He's not used to it, she thought and laughed inside, I bet he doesn't often get dismissed so casually.

'Would you mind if I give you my number?' There was that lovely smile again. 'That way you know I won't pester you, but you can contact me if you'd like to come to that party or maybe we could just go out for a drink sometime, or a go for a walk.'

She opened the contacts folder on her phone and

handed it to him, keeping an eye on Andrea, who was standing by the alcove table scanning the room, and as soon as he handed the phone back she said a casual "Bye!" and headed across the room.

Andrea was goggle eyed with excitement and curiosity. 'Did you just give that gorgeous hunk your number? Who is he? I've never seen him in here before,' she said as soon as they were seated.

'His n-name is Greg somebody, l-let me have a l-look.' She checked her contacts. 'No, he just entered Greg and his n-number. Yeah, he's utterly g-gorgeous, but I'm not sure about him, a b-bit too sure nobody would ever t-turn him down.' To avoid having a conversation about Greg while he was possibly watching them from across the room, and with Andrea's eyes inevitably swivelling his way when his name was mentioned, she got up. 'I'll g-get our d-drinks, what will you have?'

She returned and found Andrea on the phone, once again with her mother, and she could tell from the tone of her voice, slightly impatient. When the call ended she said gently, 'You sounded quite short with your l-lovely mum. Was she b-being p-particularly repetitive?'

'She's got hung up on something the new neighbours complained about the other day, and she thinks we'll have to move! I mean, honestly! They make a comment *once* about where she parks on the street next to their driveway, and she's already making plans to move! She'll drive dad crazy, you know what she's like when she gets a bee in her bonnet.'

'Why does she p-park on the street?' Mary took a sip of her wine and tried to hide a smile.

'Oh, it's just very occasionally, like when Jim comes over and parks in our driveway before she gets home from work, so she can't get in. There's not much room between our driveway and the neighbours, so last week they found it hard to reverse out. But you know what she's like – this idea that we'll have to move is becoming an obsession.'

Mary smiled. 'S-still a great mum, though! Always c-concerned about others and helping p-people.'

She got a ride home with Andrea, who these days lived in the little flat at the back of her parent's house after a sad break-up the previous year, when her partner of three years had cheated on her and she had discovered it was not the first time but one of many. Andrea hadn't dated anyone since, and Mary sometimes wondered if she would ever get over it. They sat in the car for half an hour talking about the jobs Mary had applied for, and she quickly realised that Andrea didn't understand her rationale for saying she would apply for a clerical job in amongst the very few science jobs available.

'There are very f-few jobs in chemistry right now,' said Mary. 'And n-nothing in my line available at Tidewell's and I've always wanted to work there - they d-do such interesting things. So I thought I m-might learn things even in their admin department.'

'Hmm,' said Andrea thoughtfully. 'Well, when you apply, don't leave out things that would make you seem overqualified for the admin position, will you? So many people do that, thinking that employers are reluctant to hire people who might be too clever for the job. But for Tidewell's you should include your degree, even if is a clerical role. Who knows what might turn up? You could spend a year there while you work out if you want to do a master's degree, and in that year something might become available. And if it does you'll be in the perfect position - onsite and available and you can apply as soon as you hear about it.'

'Exactly m-my thinking, and it's also and an opportunity to work out what topic to d-do my master's thesis on. I think I'll have to be very strategic b-because what I choose will set me on the right p-path for my future career.'

'You're so focused, you cute little thing.' Andrea laughed. 'I know people underestimate you when they first meet you, like that handsome hunk tonight probably did. Remember that guy last year who was so patronising and talked down to you at Ava's place when you made a comment about steroids. He thought he knew more than you - and you put him right in no uncertain terms. That was so funny!'

They both laughed and when Mary opened the car door to get out, Andrea added, 'That colour on you is very effective, stunning!'

2

After considering carefully for a week or two, Mary decided not to call or text Greg, the handsome man from the bistro. Always in the back of her mind was the thought that she might once again have encountered someone who was just interested in the abduction, even though she hadn't told him her surname and he hadn't met her before. There had been one or two sneaky attempts in the past – men attracted to the crime rather than to her as a person. A couple of years ago, the brother of one of her friends at university had asked her out on a date, and the experience had been disturbing. He suggested a walk on the newly upgraded path along the river, and she had only realised when they were having tacos at the famous Taco Trailer that there was a subtext to this date- he was avid for intimate details about her past. It was only in retrospect that she linked that little mental background noise, which she had picked up from him, with this devious attempt to find out more about what had happened to her.

She had to admit his approach was quite subtle and seemed innocuous at first. He casually brought up the fact that his mother had mentioned the abduction twenty years earlier when she heard the surname Lintott, and Mary had changed the subject after acknowledging that it had indeed happened to her. She thought he had understood that she was reluctant to talk about it, but he had reverted to the subject twice over the next half hour, despite Mary's attempts at diversion. And then in a last attempt he asked her outright if the man, who took her, had sexually violated her, and the tone of nearly hidden excitement in his voice made her feel sick, so she got to her feet, put the paper plate with her half-finished taco on the park bench and left without a word. He followed and said he was sorry, but she just held her hand out towards him, palm out, and walked away. It was very rare that anyone tried to pry, but on the occasions it happened she had found herself literally bereft of speech, unable to get a single word out.

This speech blockage had started when a police specialist tried to talk to her after she was found, and her father had refused to let the session continue when he saw how frightened she was when they asked questions about the man, who had taken her, and what he had done. She only found out many years later that her father refused to let them talk to her again and only passed on to the police what she gradually told him and her brothers over the weeks that followed.

Aside from the little humming noise in her brain she couldn't explain why she now linked the taco episode to Greg, but the slight hint of an ulterior motive from their meeting remained in her mind. But as sometimes happens, fate stepped in and a few days after her job interview, when she had just heard that she had got the clerical job at Tidewell Research, she met him by chance outside a café in Rule Street when she was on her way back to her car after a dental appointment.

'Well, look who's here - it must be my lucky day!' said Greg, smiling widely, when he realised who was coming towards him. 'Let's have a coffee if you have time and if you're not meeting anyone.'

She agreed, after a brief hesitation, which she knew he had noticed, and told herself not to be so suspicious. He seemed genuinely delighted to see her and that inkling of an underlying motive from their first meeting in the bistro was neither here nor there, perhaps he was just put off by her stammer after all, or he might have had something else on his mind. They sat at one of the little tables outside and after a few minutes she relaxed and began to enjoy his sense of fun, the way his smile made her smile too, and how nice it was to meet a man who enjoyed reading. I was being silly, she chided herself, I'm overly sensitive and I need to stop being so self-protective.

Greg did most of the talking, which didn't surprise her. He was that sort of guy, chatty and friendly, and there were no awkward pauses. He asked if she had a day off, seeing she was out with time on her hands on a weekday, and she told him she was just about to start a job at Tidewell's and asked what his job was.

'At the moment I'm involved in a series of interviews that are going to be on a psychology channel on YouTube,' he said enthusiastically. 'I'm not a specialist of any kind – I'm just the interviewer, asking questions of psychologists. I've done similar things before, being the front person and talking to clever people, a little series of interviews, but this one based on psychology is by far the most interesting.'

'Questions f-from the public or questions you m-make up?' she asked and noticed a woman at the table behind Greg holding a phone up, as if she was taking a photo of something. 'How does it work?'

'We have a topic for each interview, you know, like a theme – it was fear of snakes in the last one. We worked out the kind of questions to ask, the sort of things the general public might wonder about, and then the producer found a man with snake phobia, or maybe she'd picked that topic because she already knew him – I didn't ask.' He laughed. 'So I interviewed the phobic guy about it, and then we compiled a raft of interesting questions to ask a psychologist – like can someone be weaned off snake phobia, are there any reliable snake phobia treatments, and how do they work. It's very interesting.'

'T-turn around,' said Mary, suddenly alerted to the fact that the woman with the phone was still holding it up. 'There's a woman b-behind you and I think she's filming us. Do you know her?'

In a split second she knew the answer and got to her feet staring at him in silent fury. He hadn't even needed to turn around, the look on his face told the story without him having said a word in response, a revealing mixture of guilt and embarrassment.

'Listen,' he said quickly. 'Please listen, let me explain! We're very keen to do a couple of episodes about child abductions and the lasting impact on victims. Please don't leave! This might be valuable for you too, on a personal level, I mean.'

Mary turned to leave, but after a couple of steps she pulled her phone out of her pocket and turned to take a photo of the woman at the table behind Greg, then she moved her hand a fraction and took one of Greg too. The look on his face would have made her laugh, if she hadn't been so angry.

'Please, Mary, just listen!' he said again and got up from his chair, but the words were spoken to her back. She was already walking away fast hoping he wasn't going to follow her. When she reached her car she turned on the central locking and sat there for a few minutes until her mind cleared, and she felt calm, then she called Richard.

'I know he's p-probably with a client,' she said to the receptionist, 'but can you t-tell me if there's a gap in his schedule this afternoon? Like f-fifteen minutes, or so?'

'This is his last client for the day, but the appointment might run over time. I think he'll probably be free to call you about quarter past four, if that's OK. Oh, good! I'll tell him as soon as he comes out.'

Home again and in her room with the door shut Mary waited for Richard's call with a stream of questions lining up in her mind. Had this been a set-up? Had Greg somehow found out where she was going, had he followed her? Had their meeting in the bistro been an engineered thing? And if it was, how had it been done?

She sifted through possibilities, discarded some and made a mental note of others that she needed to ask Richard about. After a while she turned on her laptop and searched for 'tracking apps' and read one disturbing article after another. With a YouTube video playing on the laptop screen and the phone in her hand she went through the recommended steps to find out if someone had planted a tracker on her phone, but she found nothing.

'What's wrong, Mopsy?' asked Richard an hour later. 'Has something happened to dad?'

It nearly made her laugh in the middle of her worries. 'Why do you think something's happened to dad? Honestly, Rick, what a weird idea. No, he's just fine, he's playing golf in a veteran's tournament today and tomorrow.'

Richard chuckled. 'You won't believe this, and please don't tell anyone, but last night I had a very realistic dream about dad having a heart attack, and then you called the clinic and asked me to call back, which is very unusual. I don't think you've ever done that before, so I got worried.'

'You know a lot of IT stuff,' she said instead of commenting on this unusual statement from a qualified trauma counsellor, who had never before displayed any even remotely paranormal beliefs. 'You always sort out all our mysterious problems with phones and laptops and things. How quickly can someone put a tracking app on a phone? Can it be done in a minute or so? And is there some certain way of making sure there isn't one on a phone? And can they be kind of hidden, so they're not obvious.'

'What the fuck? Is someone stalking you?' Mary's eyes opened wide. She had never heard Richard swear before; he was the most laid-back of her brothers, always soft-spoken and calm.

'I'll tell you what happened,' she said and tried hard to sound relaxed, so he wouldn't get too worried. 'It's a bit of a story. It started a couple of weeks ago when I was meeting Andrea in the French Bistro where we often go, well, nearly inevitably, if we're not meeting at our place. A guy bumped into me quite hard outside the toilets – not in the passage to the toilets, just at that end of the bar and it seemed like a genuine accidental thing. And he apologised and we had a chat while I waited for Andrea, who was late. He's a charming guy, very entertaining, and then he suggested he'd put his phone number in my phone, so I could decide if I wanted to meet up for a drink or something at a later date. Which seemed like a nice way of doing things. So I handed him my phone and then I got distracted because I saw Andrea come in and start looking around for me, and I was hoping she wasn't getting worried about where I'd got to. So I probably didn't watch my phone or think of how long it was in his hand. He might have had it for a minute or a bit more.' She paused and thought. 'Oh yeah, and I've checked the app folder, but I can't find anything that looks suspicious.'

After a moment's silence Richard said, 'OK, he could have done it. For someone, who knows how to find the right app online, it's very simple. Say he's done this before, and he's picked one in advance that has some innocent sounding name. So he uploads it on your phone and when you check your app folder it doesn't register for what it is when you look for it because the name of it is so innocuous. Or maybe he's changed the icon for it to something innocent sounding – I haven't done it, but I think it can be done. But something else must have happened since then. Why are you suddenly thinking he might have put a tracker on your phone?'

Telling him about today's meeting with Greg and what he had said didn't take long and Mary concluded the story by repeating her questions about tracking apps. 'So, do you think he could have put a tracker on my phone, and how would I know? I've looked, but I haven't found anything suspicious.'

'Pull up Microsoft Teams on your laptop and log on to our group. I want you to have the phone in your hand while we talk about this, so you're ready to do what I tell you and you can show me the phone screen if necessary. OK?'

'Yes! I've deleted it,' said Mary twenty minutes later, after following Richard's instructions step by step, going down a couple of dead-ends and then finally finding where the tracking app was hidden. Not in her app folder but deviously tucked away. 'My God, that creep! If I ever see him again I'll tell him what I think about him. I feel really good now, Rick – it proves my first impression was right when I felt there was some kind of underlying motive behind his interest.'

Richard laughed quietly. 'This time, yes, but you're so damn gorgeous anyone would be interested in you. I'm glad we got this sorted. I'll see you next weekend for James's thirtieth. Are we going to Westmoreland's for dinner as usual? Did you book it?'

'Of course, it's all organised. I did it ages ago, so we'd be able to have the bigger of their private rooms, the one with corner windows that dad likes. More space for the kids to run around when they get bored. And James is bringing a new woman, and they're staying in a motel!'

They both grinned at the implied reason for this plan, then Mary closed Teams and sat for a while with her phone in her hand, thinking back to the way Greg had been so charming in the bistro. She didn't know if the story about the psychology channel on YouTube was true, but on reflection she decided it probably was. Either that or he was a journalist or blogger out to use her for his own gain or fame.

When her father came home from golf she didn't mention what had happened. Like her brothers he was very protective of her and now there was no need to worry him. In the future she would be very careful not to let others use her phone.

3

A couple of days later Mary's phone issued a text message alert when she and her father were in the kitchen. She turned from the bench and glanced at it and continued telling him about the employment agreement Tidewell's had email to her that morning.

'Don't you want to check that?' asked Archie and gestured at the phone which was on the kitchen table, and she laughed. 'Oh, no, it's nothing important, just someone from the MAMA group.'

Her father looked quizzically at her. 'You belong to a mama group now? But you're not a mama yet.'

She laughed. 'It's that little bunch of us who get together for a drink now and then, two girls from school and one mate from university. It's our initials, Mary, Ava, Maylene and Andrea. MAMA. I'll look at it later.'

She turned back to the steak and kidney pie she was making, her dad's favourite, and said over her shoulder, 'But if they want to go back to that new bar down beside the river I'm not joining them. We went there once a few weeks ago, and the place was full of women with huge false eyelashes and the type of guys who shave their chests, and literally everyone had a phone in their hands. It's supposed to be the place to go right now, because they nearly always have a live band, but it's not my scene at all. Too noisy, if nothing else.'

She started pressing the pastry down around the edges of the pie and heard her father's snort of derision behind her. 'Guys who shave their chests! God no, if you're looking for a man, look for a real one.'

'Oh, don't worry! That kind isn't for me. I've been brought up with my brothers as the blueprint for what a real man is.'

'I should hope so!' Her father went back to the newspaper and Mary, brushed the pie with beaten egg and put it in the oven. 'I've set the timer, dad. Can you have a look when it pings and see if it looks OK? Maybe stick the meat thermometer into the middle and do a scientific assessment?'

She loved teasing him about the thermometer, which he'd bought the previous year to, "do things based on science, not just a hunch," as he had said at the time, a man who liked to get his facts right. He also liked to ridicule the way some recipes said to add a pinch or a sprinkle of something – it made her laugh at how indignant he'd get. 'What the hell is a pinch?' he'd said. 'Tell me in grams, please or at least in teaspoons.'

Walking down the hall to her room she thought once again how strange it would seem to people who didn't know their family - the two of them living in this huge 1920s villa with six bedrooms, four of them empty now. But one or two of her six brothers would turn up in a random sequence and simply go back to their childhood bedrooms, now equipped with new king sized beds instead of one or two singles and two of them with sets of bunks. Three of the six were married, so when they all turned up, including four children, soon to be five, the place was full to the rafters, parents shared their bed with one or two children and sometimes Mary would wake up in the night and find a warm little body next to her in the bed like a surprise present.

Two nights later she was in another favourite bistro with the other three in the MAMA group, listening to Andrea telling them about her mother's frustration with Andrea's brother, Jim. 'She goes on about it all the time, endless moaning about how Jim and Sara always go to stay with Sara's family, and then dad says, that's how it works, it always did. Girls bring husbands back to their families more often, it's a mother-daughter thing.'

Ava laughed, reached for a potato wedge from the bowl in the centre of the table and pointed it at Mary. 'Apart from your brothers who seem to return here all the time like they're tethered with elastic bands and just get pulled back. Or maybe you've put a spell on them?'

'For God's sake, don't tell my mum!' Andrea gave a mock shudder. 'Then she'll worry even more and imagine it's something she did wrong when she brought Jim up. But I must admit it's taken her mind off having to move after the neighbours asked her not to block their driveway. I should be grateful for small mercies. I really don't know how my dad lasted so long!'

'And m-my brothers, the m-married ones, go b-both ways,' said Mary, trying to balance the discussion. 'Not quite every second t-time, but that's only b-because they feel they have to come and give me hugs and check up on me.'

'Probably checking they don't need to do another line-up.' Ava chuckled. 'Like if someone had insulted you or something.'

Mary laughed, because whenever her brothers were mentioned, the episode locally known as the Lintott line-up popped automatically into everyone's head. It had become part of local folk lore and would probably be passed down from one generation to the next, as her dad had said once.

'You should be so grateful they look after you.' Maylene made a sad face. 'My brother couldn't care less about looking after me. He'd only pay serious attention to me if I had two wheels and a big engine, I think. Ever since he bought that motor bike he's been impossible and now he doesn't live with mum I hardly see him.'

At the end of the evening Andrea and Mary caught the same bus and as usual, Andrea planned to get off at Mary's stop and walk the last part of the way to where she herself lived. 'You d-don't have to,' Mary said now, as the bus slowed. 'I live just around the c-corner, it's a t-two minute walk for me to get home, but you have to walk for at l-least ten or fifteen m-minutes to get to your place.'

'But I want to,' said Andrea. 'My mum gave me strict instructions when you started school, remember? I was to walk right beside you, on the street side of the sidewalk, hold your hand and not let go until we were at the school or at your gate.' She laughed because she knew exactly what Mary would reply.

'And now we're b-both in our twenties and we b-both still l-live at home! You're such a staunch f-friend. At least now you don't need to hold my hand.'

'God, it's cold tonight! This spring has been so weird. And who was that guy at the bar who kept staring at you?' Andrea turned up the collar on her jacket as the bus drove away. 'Had you met him before?'

'Never saw him in m-my life before, and I hope I n-never see him again. Do you want to know what he s-said when I walked p-past on the way to the restroom? He t-turned on his stool and asked if I needed "someone who knows how to satisfy"! And I knew f-from the l-look on his face what he meant.'

'He's a creep!' said Andrea dismissively. 'What a terrible pick-up line, I bet that never works. Did you stare him down? I knew he'd said something - I was watching as you walked past him because of how he'd been looking at you.'

'I ignored him,' said Mary. 'He m-might have taken any k-kind of response as an excuse to start a c-conversation.'

When she got home her father had gone to bed, but the lights were on in the kitchen and living room. Not ready to sleep yet, Mary made a cup of tea and opened a packet of shortbread biscuits. She sat in the living room to read for an hour before she went to bed, but her mind was on the past and the book remained unopened on her knees. Looking absentmindedly at the flames behind the glass in the fireplace she replayed the Lintott line-up, as it had become known, from her first year at high school. The jokes about, and imitations of, her stammer had tormented her and made her deeply unhappy, to the point where she would sometimes refuse to go to school for a couple of days. Her father had obviously discussed the problem with the three of her brothers, who still lived at home. The youngest of them had left high school the year before she started and was an apprentice builder, the other two were at university.

Then one Friday, in the lunch hour when the school yard was full of kids, her six brothers turned up. They marched in between the brick pillars at the entrance from the street, formed a dead straight line and came forward, shoulder to shoulder, and the crowd of kids parted to let them proceed until they were right in the centre. Everyone stared, kids pushed each other and pointed, and gradually the place became completely quiet, not a voice was heard. Mary had seen them right from the start and hadn't know what was going to happen. But there had to be a reason, because this way of standing in a row, close together, was how they stood every Christmas with Mary in the centre for their father to take a photo of them. The earliest photo was when she was eleven months old and she was on twenty-one year old William's arm with her hand clutching the front of his shirt. Now she slowly approached the line, thinking that perhaps they meant for her to take her customary place in the centre, hoping this was the right thing to do, though she was still baffled by the way they had appeared when she hadn't even known they were all coming home for the weekend. As soon as she got right up to them they formed a circle around her, like a protective wall of bodies and Henry said quietly, 'We're here to show those bullies that you've got protection, Mopsy, so do you want to point out the worst ones?'

'Oh no, *please*, don't let's do that!' The idea that some would then want revenge for being singled out instantly appeared in her mind. She thought for a moment. 'But listen – when you straighten out the line again, could you look across and kind of take in the whole yard? Like scan it from side to side? And then leave?' She swivelled within the circle and smiled up at them. 'You're the best ever, I love you guys! But please don't kiss and hug me when you go, just go.' She giggled. 'Hugging would totally ruin the effect.'

And that's what they did. The circle opened and the line reformed, with Mary in the middle and her six brothers all let their eyes slowly move across the school yard from one side to the other before they broke the formation and walked away. The memory of that day was imprinted on her mind, every detail clear. The sound of Henry's voice, the way they looked to her for directions, the strong feeling of safety and protection, an indelible part of her being, now and forever.

Sometimes she thought right back to the terrible time after the abduction when she was three and a half, when the boys had taken turns holding her for days after she was found, when she was on someone's knee day and night, refusing to let them put her down. When they all took turns to feed, clean and dress her and she became part of each one of them. Six boys ranging from eight to twenty-one, ten years before they formed that famous line-up in the school yard.

The stammering that had started after the abduction, was part of her life now, probably forever, though she never stammered with her brothers or her father, only with outsiders. She had been offered speech therapy when she started primary school, but it had made no difference, and now she was used to it.

One day much later, when she and her father talked about how amazing the school event had been, and how lovely it had been when they formed that circle around her, and how safe she had felt, he said, when she told him how surprised she had been, 'Of course they came – they'll always have your back, Mopsy. Their relationship with you is different from just ordinary sibling ties, I think. It's like you're a physical part of each one of them. They brought you up, physically and mentally. I don't know if you know this, but William said once that when you hurt, they hurt too. You're very lucky.'

4

As usual, the Saturday they were celebrating James's thirtieth birthday became a swirling mass of people coming and going in and out of the house, impromptu cups of coffee, loud male voices and delighted comments on how much Mary's nieces and one nephew had grown. She heard her father saying to John that he'd better hurry up if he was going to create his own family line-up with only one child so far, and was just about to comment, when Henry interrupted her with a question about coffee capsules, and she was distracted, though she would have liked to hear John's reply. His and Sylvia's daughter Sharon was now six and Mary had wondered lately if she was going to be an only child. For someone who had grown up in a large family it seemed strange to have only one, but it might have something do to with the fact that both John and Sylvia were in the police, and both very ambitious. I bet their lives get complicated sometimes, she thought as she went to find another packet of coffee capsules in the pantry, what with shift work and strange work hours. She made a mental note to ask her dad later on what John had said, handed the box to Henry and went to the bathroom.

This form of bedlam inevitably broke out when they were all together, as they were on some birthdays, always on hers, when the whole tribe gathered, and of course, at Christmas and New Year. Three single brothers, three with partners, and a little handful of children between them, but she was used to it and had prepared and planned for these occasions since she was sixteen, when her youngest brother left home.

Their family bond was sometimes commented on, and her father always responded the same way, which was how she herself did too whenever it came up: their family was glued together by past events, so connected that sometimes they seemed to be one organism, inextricably linked by what they had been through, and constantly in touch. Her father and the six boys had raised Mary since she was a motherless ten months-old, taking turns with baby minding tasks and seeing to it that there was always someone to play with her, clean her up or comfort her if she woke in the night. Then the aftermath of the abduction had created a web of interlinked affection and protection which was nearly impossible to explain to outsiders.

Two days before the birthday party she and her father went to the supermarket when she came home from work, to shop for a succession of meals, from dinner on Friday night for those who lived close enough to come early, to lunch for the last stragglers on Sunday with varying numbers from six to thirteen, all worked out to fit with arrivals and departures at different times. The basic shopping list was saved on Mary's laptop and only need a few handwritten adjustments each time she printed it out. As usual they had half the list and a trolley each, checked out separately and met up in the car park.

'Am I getting old or is this getting more tiring each year? So many celebrations every year,' said her dad and started loading the car. 'I can't even imagine how many times you must have organised these crazy get-togethers by now. You're a logistics wizard, Mopsy.'

'So long as you don't call me logistics witch!' said Mary from where she was leaning into the car putting bags on the back seat. She heard a man chuckle behind her, then a car door closing. She glanced over her shoulder, but the car was already reversing out and the reflections in the car window meant she couldn't see who it was. She shook her head and lifted another two bags out of the trolley.

And now, on a nearly perfect Saturday morning, the large kitchen was noisy with talk and laughter, the electric jug was being refilled for the third time, and Mary was putting more mugs on the counter, more biscuit packets on the table and tried to listen to little Sharon, who had lost two front teeth and lisped on some words.

'Sorry, d-darling,' said Mary and pulled Sharon slightly to one side. 'I didn't hear that. What d-did you say?'

'I thaid, I'm going to look exactly like you when I grow up. Dad thays I look *exactly* like you did when you were six.'

And all through this slightly chaotic day, when it was impossible to talk for any length of time to anyone without being interrupted, Mary registered how quiet James's new woman friend was and wondered if she felt out of place. Not that the family ever got really dressed up to go out for dinner, but Yolanta's bright pink hair and pink boots would certainly stand out in the restaurant, as would her height, nearly as tall as James. To make sure she felt included Mary joined her by the open kitchen window after lunch was cleared away. Outside a game of cricket was in progress, as usual with both children and adults taking part and a mix of shouted instructions and comments from the terrace.

'We're a noisy l-lot,' said Mary and laughed quietly. 'That big garden is such a b-blessing seeing what a large family we are – and slowly getting b-bigger.'

Yolanta smiled. 'It's lovely! James told me it would seem like a madhouse at first, but you have no idea how wonderful this seems to me, like something out of a story. I'm an only child of a single mother and our flat was very quiet. So James warned me - but this! It's like a different world compared to how I grew up.'

'What is it you d-do? Nobody's t-told me anything.' Mary studied the large brown eyes looking seriously into hers and wondered how old Yolanta was, but probably a few years older than James.

'I'm a librarian, and so was my mother, though she retired years ago. She was an old mother, so to speak – forty-one when I was born. I might go out and help that team with two little kids, they're not doing so well.'

But then John's wife Sylvia joined them and the conversation veered off to other things, and the rest of the afternoon sped past, as time always did when they were all together.

Westmoreland's was nearly like home, thought Mary, when they arrived for the Saturday night dinner, as usual in a taxi mini-bus to avoid parking issues and having to decide which cars to take and who was going to drive home. The staff knew them all, if not by name, at least by sight, and their welcome was guaranteed. This time Mary surprised her family with a new improvement to her planning. As soon as they were seated and the menus were put in front of them she got to her feet.

'I made an executive decision,' she said looking straight into the eyes of Henry, the only sure-fire way of talking to the group without stammering, as if she was talking only to him, the way they had worked it out years before, when she found it hard to speak to the family when their girlfriends were with them. She held up her hands and counted on her fingers. 'I have taken into account one gluten intolerance, one shellfish allergy, and one intense dislike of anything hot - and one fusspot who takes ten minutes to decide on a dessert and then changes his mind in the last minute - and compiled a set menu without choices. *But* there are various side dishes to choose from and of course several desserts, but not too many.'

She grinned at Henry, who was fussy about desserts, and continued. 'The maître d' actually suggested this - based on how long it took for us to order at Henry's fortieth last year, and how many people changed their minds while listening to what others ordered. So this is a trial of a new format.'

'Always the master planner,' said John to Sylvia, who was openly laughing. 'She's been bossing us around since she was a toddler.'

At quarter to eleven they filed out of the private room and threaded their way through the main dining room, a row of eleven adults and four sleepy children, and among them six males, one woman and one little girl with the same thick, black curly hair. People's eyes followed their progress, some smiled and said something to others who then turned to look. Mary didn't notice the recognition on people's faces because this had happened so many times that it no longer registered; the Lintott family on the move as a group was hard to ignore.

The process of taking turns in the bathroom, dealing with over-tired children, and some deciding another glass of wine would be nice, took time and when Mary finally went to bed she was exhausted. She was woken at some ungodly hour of the morning when a small body clambered into her bed and settled down sideways with the top of her head touching Mary's shoulder. Breannah, she thought and smiled in the dark, she always gets in sideways for some reason. Reaching over she pulled the blanket up over the little body, put her arm over her and went back to sleep. In the morning all that was left of her nighttime visitor was a small stuffed dog abandoned beside Mary's pillow or perhaps left to keep her company. By half past seven Mary was in the kitchen, setting out an assortment of breakfast options on the table when Henry turned up. 'Oh, good – you can do the plates and things.' She gestured to what she had already got out. 'We need cereal bowls, spoons, butter knives, glasses and small plates for toast. I'll get the stuff we need from the fridge, it's so full you'd never find anything.'

By the time orange juice, milk and yoghurt was on the table and coffee mugs lined up on the counter, the kitchen had filled. Children were clamouring for their favourite cereal, the toaster was in continuous use, and Mary quietly helped herself to a slice of toast, spread peanut butter on it and went to sit at the far end of the kitchen table. This was the part of celebration weekends she enjoyed most, sitting quietly watching the chaos evolving in front of her and listening to her brothers, their partners and children. We really are a tribe, she thought, and it's constantly growing. The morning continued to be busy and fragmented with departures at intervals, bags carried out to cars, children protesting at being made to go to the toilet before getting into the car and several episodes of someone running back inside for something they had forgotten.

After lunch James and Yolanta were the last to leave and suddenly the house was silent. 'It's always the same, isn't it?' Mary's father said when he and Mary went back inside after waving them off. 'I only realise how huge this house is after they leave. When we bought it way back, must be forty-five years ago, it was cheap because it was too big for most people and very run down, and we got it for a song. The old man, who had lived here alone for several years, died and his children just wanted to get rid of it. It was listed by the real estate company with the suggestion that it should be pulled down.'

'Why?' asked Mary. 'What a strange thing to put in a sales ad.'

He grinned. 'Developers! They thought they were appealing to those who turn big pieces of land into several small ones and build houses close together for max profit. But there was an obstacle, so I was able to buy it up for very little considering what I got.'

'I bet it's the tree!' Mary started to laugh. 'You've never told me this before. How lucky that tree is protected and can't be cut down, or where would you have fitted in so many kids?'

'Not only is the tree protected,' said her dad, 'it's also in the perfect position the ruin any plans to divide the place into enough small sections to make it worthwhile. Someone said at the time that it was planted in 1912 which explains the size.'

They did what they always did after the family events, gathered up the sheets and towels and put them in the bins Mary had bought a few years ago, turned on the dishwasher and set out for the big laundromat in the next suburb, where they had huge washing machines that could take twelve kilos and equally big dryers. This routine made short work of dealing with so much washing, and they knew exactly how long the wash cycle took and went for a mid-afternoon coffee two doors down.

'We've really got this down to a fine art, haven't we?' said Mary. 'Remember years ago when we had that cleaning woman, when I was a little girl, and she used to come in and do an extra day and do all this laundry, one load after another. This is so much simpler.'

'It's all your doing – the way you've sorted things out so they can be managed. I'm very proud of you, you know.'

Mary just smiled and thought of the year when she decided to change things and told the assembled family that everyone had to strip their bed and put their sheets and towels on the floor in the laundry room before they left. The same year she had told her father to buy the bins and told him he had to drive her to the laundromat she had found online, a routine they had followed ever since.

5

Having a reserved space in the big parking building that shared a wall with Tidewell Research was a bonus Gabriel hadn't expected when he took the job, but it was very convenient. His flat was in an outer suburb which meant either taking two buses into the centre of the city or taking the car and paying excessive parking fees, neither of which was an attractive prospect. And not only was the parking building next door to his workplace, it also had direct access from the ground floor, to Tidewell's on one side and to another building on the other.

Normally he took the lift or the stairs to the ground floor after parking on level two, but this day he had been immersed in thoughts about a problem with some new software and found himself walking down the car ramps. He shook his head at himself and thought that this was exactly the kind of thing he would have labelled stupidity if he had seen someone else do it, particularly in this place that seemed to have more drivers going too fast than any other parking building he'd ever been in. His mother would love to hear about him doing this and say that he had inherited her risk taking gene after all, but he wouldn't tell her, because to her walking on the ramps in a parking building wouldn't even qualify as risk. He and his father were both cautious, apart from on the rugby field, but his mother had been a dare devil since childhood and did things that made his father close his eyes and refuse to watch. "One day you'll take a risk too many, go too far!' he would say, and Gabriel's mother would laugh. 'But think of the fun I have before I get to that point, darling – well worth it, don't you think?'

Gabriel was nearly at ground level now, ready to check for incoming vehicles before he crossed to the far side of the ramp to continue across to the door to the Tidewell reception area. As he reached into his pocket for the swipe card to open that door, there was a raucous bellow of laughter from somewhere very close. Surprised, he came to a stop and heard a raised voice say, 'Christ, Sean! Just because you failed doesn't mean one of us can't manage. She just didn't fancy your pickup line. I bet I'll have her in bed before the end of the month. Imagine that hair when she's naked – all those black curls, luscious! It might be worth putting up with the stammer, I think, or maybe I'll just tell her to shut up. You'll love the video when I post it, guys! I've got a great little gadget for holding the phone to film secretly now, can't wait to try it.'

A third one chimed in, cocky and confident. 'You're full of shit, Sniff - I'm the only one who works in the same place, so obviously I've got the best chance. You might as well give me your money right now, guys, I'm bound to win.'

Astounded Gabriel stood silent and continued listening for a few minutes as the salacious conversation continued, interspersed with bursts of laughter. I've got three names now, he told himself, but I need to see these guys, so I can point them out in the future. Or maybe I'll just intervene right now, see if I can scare the hell out of them and stop this in its tracks. He took the last few steps down the ramp, made a sharp turn left instead of heading across to the Tidewell door and found four young guys standing under the higher curve of the ramp.

He walked rapidly right up close before they noticed him and didn't stop until he was practically chest to chest with the one who swung around, his sudden approach took them totally by surprise.

'Right!' he said and swung his arm out to stop the one trying to walk away to the side. 'Let's have a chat, guys. Which one of you works for Tidewell's?'

After a slight hesitation the shortest and youngest said, 'I do.'

'And your name is?'

'Bruce.'

'Surname?'

'Carswell.'

'Do you know who I am?'

They all shook their heads, struck dumb by this sudden confrontation. 'I'm a manager at Tidewell. I presume the rest of you work for the brokerage firm in the other building?'

They nodded, still silent. Suddenly one of them turned and made as if to walk away, saying dismissively over his shoulder, 'Oh, fuck off, man! This isn't your ...'

He got no further. Before the other three could react, Gabriel had the stroppy guy's arm bent up behind his back, swung him around and said with obvious menace. 'Just a moment! I haven't finished. You lot are going to leave that girl alone! No more attempts to get her into bed – no moves in her direction at all! If I hear so much as a whisper about any approach from you I'll make sure you're all very sorry, you little shits.'

He gave the wrist he was holding an extra little upward jerk until the guy groaned in pain, let him go and walked to the Tidewell door leaving utter silence behind him. He knew the girl they talked about. He had never had a conversation with her, so the stammer was new to him. She was possibly the most gorgeous female in the building, and her hair had been commented on ever since she started at Tidewell's a few months earlier. Luxuriant, thick hair in big lose natural curls, so black it looked nearly blue in some lights. Hair the colour of a raven's wing, someone had said when she first appeared. During the rest of the day he wondered if he should report the guy called Bruce to his manager, whoever that was – Tidewell Research had nearly one hundred and fifty employees spread over several floors and some of them he couldn't place. But on consideration he decided that his size and fury had probably made them revise their plans and decided to leave it for now but keep an eye out for those guys from now on.

After several weeks at Tidewell Research Mary had become familiar with most of the layout which covered five levels in the big white building in the centre of the city, but she had never had occasion to go to the stationery room. Now she followed the directions Debbie gave her and walked down the long corridor to the right and counted doors. The fourth door was open, and the light was on showing a wide but shallow little room with shelving units in a row, their ends towards the door. From beside one unit full of what looked like computer gear came Gretchen, the receptionist.

'Oh hi, have you been in here before or do you want a guided tour? This place is such a mess, and nobody ever takes the time to sort it out.' She smiled and made a gesture towards the shelves on the far side. 'Just look at that, full of stuff that should have gone to recycling years ago.'

Mary returned her smile and thought what a nice woman she was, always friendly and helpful. 'I n-need a ream of headed A4 paper for a report we're printing. D-do you know where it is?'

'Right there on the last unit to the right, second shelf from the bottom. All the up to date stuff, which we actually use, is on the shelves on the far side.' Gretchen made a sweeping gesture. 'And some generally useful stuff over here on the next shelf. The rest is either out of date stuff that should be dumped, or spare parts for the IT guys, they've taken over the unit at that end, and their stuff seems to be slowly spreading.'

She walked past Mary, stopped in the doorway and pointed. 'And there's no light switch – just close the door and the light goes off. That little button on the door frame works the light when you open and shut the door.'

She disappeared down the corridor towards the front lobby and Mary looked around the space with a frown. Why didn't they just sort it out? Maybe as companies grew they got unwieldy, roles were less defined, and everyone just put up with things and thought it was someone else's job. She could offer to do it, but so far she had been kept very busy and had little time to do anything apart from what she was asked to do. She smiled when she remembered Debbie's face when she realised that Mary was skilled at spreadsheet work and how helpful that would be. 'That's great!' she had said with obvious relief. 'We desperately need another person on this team who can do accurate data entry and spot mistakes.'

Just when Mary bent to pick up the ream of paper, someone came in and went to the other end of the room.

She listened for a moment, gripped the pack of paper with one hand – and the light went out.

Gabriel was crouching beside a shelf with computer screens when the room became as dark as night. Carefully he felt his way to the door and ran his fingers over the wall, but there was no light switch, and the door had no handle on the inside, which was unusual. He would just have to wait until he heard footsteps outside and knock on the door to be let out, he thought and leaned against the wall, but then he heard something. A very soft sound like a small animal quietly whimpering. He moved slowly toward the far end of the room, carefully felt his way past the ends of the shelf units and cursed the fact that he didn't have his phone to light the way. Counting shelves he mentally calculated where he was, tried to recreate what he had seen when he first entered the room. Probably the sixth shelf his hand was resting on now was the last, then there was a space before the end wall, so somewhere here his feet might encounter a small, miserable obstacle. Puppy, he thought as he inched carefully forward, it sounds like an unhappy puppy, one that doesn't dare make a loud noise. But how on earth could it have ended up here?

And then he was very close to whatever it was, but the sound was not coming from the floor, and he realised it was a person, someone in deep distress. Cautiously he reached out with both hands and his left hand landed on a shoulder. The whimper became louder. Whoever this was, she was terrified, and her shoulder stiffened under his hand. 'No, no, no,' she moaned, and he did the only thing he could think of. He let his hands slip along her arms and found she was holding the edge of a shelf, leaning forward. He gripped her wrists and crossed his arms in front of her, across her midriff, holding her wrists firmly. She tensed, but he pulled her back against his chest and said quietly, 'It's OK, I'm not going to hurt you. Just lean against me and take a deep breath.'

Holding her stiff body against him he considered the options and decided the only thing he could do was continue talking to her the way one would with a frightened child. 'It's OK now,' he said, keeping his voice low. 'Nothing's going to happen, I'm here, I've got you, it's all right.'

After a couple of minutes her stance relaxed and she leaned her full weight back against his chest and just stood there, silent. The top of her head was level with his chin; he smelled the lemony scent of her shampoo. Trying to move this strange situation back to something resembling normal he said cautiously, 'Is it the dark or being locked in?'

'B-both,' she replied. 'I p-panicked. S-sorry!' Her voice was reedy, her breaths shallow.

'Let's turn you around.' Without waiting for her to reply he let go of her wrists and turned her by taking hold of her upper arms. 'Come here,' he said and pulled her in, wrapped his arms around her and held her tight. 'I know it's still dark and we're still locked in, but I'm here and I won't let go of you.'

She sighed with her face against his shoulder, a sound of deep relief that spoke volumes, and he knew he had been right; she had been truly terrified. And though he had no experience of what panic attacks were like, he wondered if maybe this had been one.

Her breathing had calmed, and as they stood there in the pitch blackness, close together and not speaking, his right hand moved as if of its own accord, up through thick curly hair and cupped her head to hold her against him. She nestled in, as if they had stood like this many times in some different past, as if they knew each other. It was a strange sensation he had never experienced before, like an unspoken conversation, communicating things they didn't need to voice.

After a few minutes she spoke, her voice muffled against his shirt, but sounding calm and without stammering. 'Do you have your phone?'

'No, we'll just have to wait.' He moved a couple of steps back and leaned against the wall, and she came with him, clearly not about to disengage from his hold, and he realised that as long as it was totally dark, she needed him to continue holding her. 'Sooner or later someone will come for something, or we'll hear footsteps in the corridor and shout at them to let us out.'

He knew who she was now. There was nobody else in the building with hair as thick and naturally curly; hair that made men turn to look as she passed. He could see her in his mind's eye. This was the girl those guys in the underground car park had been talking about.

And hot on the heels of that thought it struck him that they must somehow manage to exit separately. The nasty discussion he had overheard in the parking building came back to him in all its ugly detail. To have it known they had been locked in here for a length of time would play right into the hands of those bastards, and he could just imagine what they would say and share on social media.

'Listen,' he said after formulating a plan in his mind. 'When someone opens the door, you stay here behind this furthest bank of shelves, and I'll go and divert them, so you can slip out unnoticed. I don't want you to be subjected to stupid jokes about being locked in here with me.'

She was silent for a surprisingly long time. Gabriel waited and wondered if she was going to ask why, and in that case, what he would say.

'OK, thank you.' Silence again and he could nearly feel her hesitation before she spoke. 'I know about the bet.'

This was unexpected and intrigued he asked, 'How do you know? I overheard those little shits talking about it in the carpark the other day, and I had a go at them, but surely nobody told you directly?'

'A girl from the finance team warned me, the one with blue hair. She came to find me specially, she said they've done this before, one from here and some others who work in the building on the far side of the parking building. It's like a competition and she thinks they share their ... exploits on social media. She knows someone at that company in the other wing, who told her about it. So I'm forewarned, but ...'

'Yes? But what?'

'It makes me nervous. I feel as if I must have my back against the wall, at all times - metaphorically, I mean, like

I'm always on my guard. I know this sounds ridiculous, but it feels as if they're chasing me, or maybe pursuing me is a better way to describe it.'

He chose not to comment on this disturbing confession, because what can you say to someone who feels as if they are prey? Instead he changed the subject to something safer, less emotional. 'Hey, you've stopped stammering. Was it just the fear?'

Now the silence on her part lasted even longer until she said slowly, and her tone made it clear that she could hardly believe what she was saying, 'I *always* stammer, *always!* Apart from with my dad and my brothers. How odd!'

He couldn't help it; he tightened his arms just a fraction and chuckled. 'Well done, you! You're locked in a dark room, and you've stopped stammering.'

'Oh, it won't have stopped. It will start again when I talk to others.' She sighed. 'Like when I've been with my brothers, and then I go and talk to someone else and there it is, back again.'

He didn't know if he should acknowledge how much she had just revealed. Perhaps he should pretend the implication of his part in this had gone over his head and not comment, but then he thought she might find that insulting.

'I'm very pleased that you feel safe with me. Thank you for telling me – it makes me feel quite special.'

'You are,' she said simply. 'Very special, the first person ever outside my family.'

And then, just as he thought he heard her giggle quietly,

as if she had just thought of something funny, someone spoke outside the door.

'Stay here!' Gabriel released her and made sure she was standing stably after being supported for so long before he walked quickly towards the far end of the room, feeling for the ends of the shelf units to guide him. As he passed the door it opened and the light came on, and he said loudly, 'Thank God! I've been locked in for quite a while in total darkness.'

Then another voice, which Mary recognised as the boy with the Scottish accent from the IT department, the one who had come to set up her logon when she started. 'Really? Doesn't this door open from inside? Isn't that daft? What are you doing here?'

'I came to look for a second screen - I like to have two. Someone said there's a stash of left over computer gear here, so I came to see what I could find seeing I was on this level anyway. Some of this stuff must have been here for years, it's ancient.'

'Yeah, when I first started here we had a manager who was very reluctant to get rid of any gear and since then nobody's tackled it. We should send a lot of this to the tech recycling place, and they even take the cables now – they strip them. But I don't think any of the screens here are much good, and they're all small. You probably want a big one.'

Their voices sounded different now and came from the far side of the shelves with computer equipment, so while they discussed what they found, Mary slipped silently out and went to the restroom two doors down the corridor.

Looking at herself in the mirror she marvelled at how calm she looked. No sign of those horrible minutes when panic had taken over her mind and obliterated reason and thought, before whatever-his-name-was had grabbed hold of her. And only then did she realise that she had no idea of who he was, not even what he looked like. She had never seen his face, and all she knew was that he was tall and strong – and kind. She waited ten minutes, and when she ventured out into the corridor they had left, so she picked up the ream of paper she had come for, while on high alert and ready to shout in case someone came past and shut the door again.

'Oh, there you are - was it hard to find?' Debbie took the packet of paper from her and went to put it beside the copier, talking over her shoulder. 'That room is a disaster zone. We should do a stock take so we know when we're about to run out of things and we should also organise a little working bee and sort it out, one day when we don't have anything to do, ha-ha!'

'No, I got d-delayed because Gretchen gave me a t-tour of what's there – and then I couldn't find the headed p-paper where she told me to look - sorry to k-keep you waiting.' She had to lie, she couldn't possibly tell anyone what had happened in the stationery room. It felt very private, and she still hadn't quite sorted out in her mind what the ability to speak to a stranger without stammering meant. It had never happened before, not even with her brothers' partners or her best friends, so in some way it was significant, but why?

'It's OK, Graham is still busy, but as soon as he's free you two can get on with the copying.'

After some hesitation Mary decided to tell her dad a heavily edited version of what had happened with no mention of the stationery room. She was well aware that her entire tribe of males, all seven of them, had wondered if she would ever feel safe enough with anyone apart from themselves to speak without stammering. They had probably stopped discussing it. It was a long time since she'd overheard it mentioned, but it would be nice for her father to hear that it could happen. So that night over dinner, she brought the subject up when he happened to mention her friend Andrea, which seemed like a good lead-in without her bringing it up out of the blue.

'I bumped into Andrea's mother in the supermarket today,' he said. 'My goodness that woman is exhausting, isn't she? A good person but imagine living with endless repetitions all day! She just can't stop telling you the same thing over and over.'

Mary laughed. 'Did she tell you about possibly having to move after the new neighbours talked to her about parking her car too close to their driveway? Andrea said that this time she'll probably drive her dad insane. Lucky that Andrea lives in the granny flat and not actually in the house with them.' She paused for a short moment. 'And talking about Andrea ... you know how I've sometimes wondered why I still stammer when I talk to her. Even though I trust her as if she's part of the family. And sometimes I've thought maybe it will always be just you and the boys I don't stammer with. But today I met someone I don't stammer with, a guy at work I hadn't talked to before.'

Her father gave her a searching look across the kitchen table. 'That's strange – but nice! I wonder why? If you hadn't talked to him before it can't be just about trust. Do you have a theory, and did it last? I mean right through a conversation?'

'He rescued me when I nearly fell, took hold of me from behind. He doesn't work on my floor, so I hadn't met him before. We only had a short exchange, maybe four or five sentences, but the stammer didn't come back.'

She lay awake a long time that night and relived the stationery room episode, tried to recall every detail. The way she had jumped when he took hold of her wrists and pulled her back against him, his calm voice saying she was safe, then that little quiet sentence, "let's turn you around" followed by being clasped against his chest. The feeling of safety and protection, the way his hand slipped up through her hair and curved around her skull to keep her firmly anchored against his shoulder. Her face buried in his shirt and the smell of his warm skin, and how he talked quietly and slowly, telling her that everything was all right. And then, best of all, he leaned back against the wall, and she revelled in that strong body holding her tight, the way he just stood there supporting her weight, solid and reliable.

And she had talked to him without stammering after the first couple of sentences. Incredible, she thought sleepily. Like a guardian angel. And now, what would happen when they met again, as they were nearly bound to? Would he know who she was and say something?

7

Over the next couple of weeks Mary's thoughts kept returning to the man in the stationery room, speculating about him and then telling herself to be sensible and just forget about him, but it hadn't managed to dismiss him from her mind. She found herself pausing in the middle of a task at work or at home and simply stand there, while her mind once again plagued her with questions. Who was he and how could she find him? How to identify who he was among all those people who worked at Tidewell's. At least half of them were men, probably more, and she couldn't in real life walk up to each one and sniff his skin, so she must work out something else. If there were approximately eighty-five men working in the building then probably only twenty were as tall as the man in the stationery room, perhaps even fewer. One night when she couldn't sleep she had an idea and the next morning she started a little campaign of speaking to every male of the right height to whom she could reasonably say something.

Even if it was only "sorry, I didn't see you" after pretending to nearly bump into someone or asking a man, who got into the lift after her, which floor he wanted. At the end of four days she had managed to speak a little short sentence to three men and stammered with each one she spoke to. Finding the man from the stationery room by this method might take a long time, but it was the only thing she had come up with, so more planning was needed.

Mary's family home was a huge wooden house built over a hundred years ago by a wealthy merchant with a large family, as was common in those days. Her parents had altered parts of it long before she was born; converted one of the seven bedrooms to a second bathroom and combined the original kitchen with what had been the dining room, in itself a big room. This large space was the centre of family living, a big L-shaped room with a long kitchen table, and in the shorter arm of the L-shape two old sofas, the TV and a couple of armchairs, perfect for informal living. But the room, which was always referred to as the old living room, was Mary's favourite room in the house. It had been untouched since the house was built, a large perfectly square room flooded with light from wood framed French doors opening onto the deck and the back garden, with tall windows on each side of the doors and a perfect view right down to the tall trees at the far end. This was where someone would sit to be quiet, to recover from a busy day and maybe listen to music or read, when the kitchen, as they called it, was busy with cooking and people sitting talking around the table.

The old sitting room was a sanctuary not often used.

This was where her father sometimes played cards or sat down over a drink with his friends, and where the annual Christmas photo was taken of the seven siblings lined up in front of the large brick fireplace. One night when her father was out with friends, Mary sat curled up in the corner of the sofa, looking abstractedly out over the garden, and tried to think what else she could do to find the man from the stationary room. She had resigned herself and admitted that she was unable to stop wondering about him, and the idea that she could find him by speaking to men of the right height had not paid off. If anyone had told her how hard it would be to quickly think up a random little sentence to say to someone, just to see if she could do it without stammering, she would never have believed it. It had seemed like a perfectly simple thing to do, but it was actually quite hard, and she had missed several opportunities by hesitating. The fact that when, or if, she found him, she might also find that he was married or had a girlfriend made no impression on her obsession. In her mind it was perfectly clear that he was destined to be a significant person in her life, or why had she been able to talk fluently to him? She hesitated to even think it, but she felt he belonged to her, or maybe she belonged to him. A disturbing idea to have about someone she had spent fifteen minutes with and whose face she had never seen, but in her mind this thought had a life of its own and persisted, however hard she tried to push it to one side.

After a while she got up and wandered around the room, absent-mindedly running a hand along the back of the armchairs, then along the piecrust edge of the sideboard while her mind continued to obsess about her situation. She crossed the hallway to the kitchen and made a cup of green tea with a teaspoon of honey and turned the TV on, determined to distract herself and sat down to watch a Korean rom-com she had read about that morning.

'You seem distracted,' said her dad over dinner a couple of days later. 'Is something bothering you?'

She hadn't realised that her constant dwelling on the unknown man was so obvious, so now she must somehow come up with some explanation so he wouldn't worry. 'Well, yes,' she said and took a sip of water to give herself another few seconds to think. 'I'm still thinking of doing my master's degree and what topic I might choose. I've got to start in good time if I'm going to do it, there are so many parts to it. First I have to find a mentor and present my idea for a thesis subject for him or her to approve, and I want that person to be someone with a really great reputation in their specialist field. But I'm really only interested in two subjects.'

'Let me guess. Something involving rDNA is one of them?'

'Yep – and the other is enzymes, particularly those linked to liver function. I can probably find someone to mentor me for either of those, but the senior people who have the best reputation for either of those aren't at our university here. One of the best is in Wellington and one in Auckland. And you know how reluctant I am to live in the North Island, so far from everyone.'

She knew this diversionary tactic would create a discussion that easily explained her distracted state, and they spent the next hour debating the pros and cons of either finding someone in the South Island or changing to a different topic for her thesis and what that might mean if she then decided to go on to a doctorate.

'But don't worry about it, dad,' said Mary when they finally sat down to watch a re-run of the TV news. 'I don't *have* to have the best there is, and as you said, being closer to all of you is probably the most important thing. I'll spend some time asking questions of some post-grad students I know before I make a decision. I just need to get some more advice.'

But it was harder to divert her own mind from dwelling on the problem of how to find that man, than it was to divert her father's concern. So single-minded had she been that it was only late one night when she was cleaning her teeth that she met her own eyes in the mirror and groaned at herself. She had got so absorbed in this quest that she had completely overlooked the fact that to him she was nothing, just someone who had panicked, someone he had been kind to. This bond she felt was one-sided. He wouldn't feel the kind of connection she felt, maybe he was married and had a family. Perhaps he did think of her now and then and felt pleased that she had stopped stammering when they talked, but not in a way that would obsess him, more like a fleeting thought now and then, pleased that he had been useful. So even if she did find him, they would be casual strangers with no significant connection.

She spat toothpaste into the basin and told herself she was being an idiot, went to bed with a newly loaded book on her Kindle and promptly started thinking about him again. Could she remember anything that might identify him? He was tall, probably about the same height as William. He was kind, and he smelt good and had lovely warm hands. She remembered how safe she had felt when his hand clasped the back of her head and anchored her against his shoulder, but she had nothing definitive to help in her search. She didn't know what colour his hair was, how old he was or even what kind of clothes he wore. 'He belongs to me!' she whispered to herself and turned the bedside light off. 'I need him, he's mine. I've got to find him.'

8

More and more people crowded into the lift, and everyone kept moving back to make room. Mary was right at the back, but at least she was in the corner where she had a bit more space. In front of her was a wall of backs, people taller and broader who hemmed her in and completely blocked her view. Finally a last couple of guys got in, she couldn't see them, but their conversation came with them in the door.

'Christ no!' said one. 'I'll let Gregory have a go, it's his turn to try. She's gorgeous, and I love the hair, but the stammer! Imagine that in the middle of sex – totally off-putting.'

'For God's sake!' exclaimed a woman somewhere towards the front of the lift. 'Would you two morons shut up! How dare you have that kind of conversation in a lift?'

Total silence followed and suddenly Mary realised that the man in front of her had taken a step back and she was now pressed into the corner, her nose nearly touching his shirt.

It's him! I know his smell, now I'll be able to talk to him! Excited she moved a little without intending to, but his left arm swung back slowly until his hand found her arm and he grasped her wrist in a gentle, but steady grip. Barely moving his head, he said quietly over his shoulder, 'Stay there!'

Standing immobile she waited, with his body very close hiding her from everyone. The lift stopped at the third floor, and more than half the people got out. She could sense that those two guys had left, but the man in front of her didn't move aside and still blocked her in the corner. When the lift stopped on level four he let his hand drop and moved forward, and she followed even though this wasn't where she worked. As soon as they were out of the lift she reached out and touched his arm, and he stopped. 'Please don't go! I knew it was you, I could smell ...'

He turned to face her and her breath caught in her throat. He was the man with the scar! She had seen him around a few times and each time she wondered how he got the scar, which made him look completely different depending on which side you looked at. One side was handsome and friendly looking, but from the other side he looked dangerous, like a thug. A big, strong man with a disfiguring scar running at an angle from the outer corner of his eye to the jaw, a lumpy scar of a kind she had never seen before.

'What could you smell?' He was amused and she realised she had said too much. She felt her face go hot and knew that now she must explain. 'I could smell you – I know you're the man who was in the stationery room.' She knew she didn't have to explain who she was. He had obviously known she was just behind her in the lift, but how he knew who she was, she couldn't imagine.

'Do I smell bad?' He sounded surprised and a bit confused.

'No, no,' she said quickly. 'God, no, of course you don't! I meant I know what your skin smells like from when ... from the stationery room.'

The look he gave her was disbelieving, and if it hadn't been from the little upward twist of humour at the corner of his mouth she would have left in disarray at having embarrassed herself so thoroughly. 'I can tell my brothers apart in the dark, and my dad,' she said quickly, 'just by how their skin smells. You smell ...'

'Yes?'

'Nice,' she said and started to laugh. This was the strangest conversation she'd ever had, strange and embarrassing, but also funny. 'I'm so sorry, I've done this all wrong. Please don't feel offended. Every one of my brothers would tell me off for being so personal.'

'How many brothers do you have? Three?'

'Six!'

Now he laughed too. 'So it's no mean feat to be able to tell them apart in the dark then - what an unusual skill.'

He made a slight move as if he was about to walk away and suddenly near panic gripped her. She must keep him there a bit longer, have a proper conversation. 'Oh, please don't go! I've been trying to work out who you are. You saved me that day.' She looked seriously up at his face, intent on not letting him walk away. She felt very strongly that there was an unspoken conversation they needed to revisit. 'If you hadn't been there I would have been a screaming heap on the floor by the time that IT guy came along.'

His face told her nothing, only that he was considering something, she could nearly see the cogs moving in his head. 'You're still not stammering.'

She hadn't realised and confused by the fact that the effect had lasted all this time, and also that he had noticed, she realised he was right.

'Oh, I do, but only with other people, not with you, so it's probably permanent.' After a second she added, 'I told my dad I didn't stammer with you, but I didn't tell him about being locked in with you. He couldn't believe it. They all thought I'd never be able to un-stammer myself with anyone outside the family. I even stammer with my best friends and my sisters-in-law and my nieces and nephews.'

Impulsively she added, 'I only speak like this with people who really belong to me, so now you do too.' Then she held her breath while she waited to hear what he would say to this outrageous statement. Did he realise now that there was a closer than normal bond that linked them? That to her he was special, important in a very significant way?

After another pause while he studied her face, he said unexpectedly, 'Hold out your hand.'

Surprised she held out her right hand, palm up, and he

pulled something out of his pocket. 'This is for you.' With one of his hands under hers he put something small on her palm and closed her fingers over it. 'For when you're in the dark and I'm not around to ...'

She opened her fingers and saw that he had given her a little flat disk of dark grey stone, about the size of a two dollar coin, perfectly smooth, nearly polished looking.

'It's warm.'

'It's been in my pocket. It's special, a stone coin.'

'How is it special? Is it magical?' She couldn't believe this was happening. It felt intimate, as if they were alone in a private space, as if they knew each other and could say anything. People were walking past and around them, there were voices and footsteps, but they were in a bubble of private conversation, a very personal conversation.

'I found it years ago on a walk, and I often carry it when I have a particularly tiresome meeting to sit through, like today. Something to fiddle with without being obvious when I get bored. It's soothing. Maybe it will help you.'

'Are you meaning that I should keep it?'

'Of course, it's for you to hold when you feel ... let's say off-balance, to help you stay calm. But I must go, or I'll be late.'

He turned on his heel and walked away and left her standing there, touched and confused in equal measure. She shook her head, got into the lift when it next stopped and went down to the admin department. For the rest of the day her hand would steal into her pocket, touch the stone to make sure it was still there, and the way he had held her in the dark would come back like a nearly physical sensation. His strong arms around her, his chin touching the top of her head, his warm chest. I want him, she thought, I really want him, he's wonderful.

The next morning she managed to casually introduce the man with the scar in a conversation with Debbie. 'Could you go and check this with Markus on the third floor, please. He's just down to the left of the stairs in the big open office. I think you met him when you first started here. He's not replied to my email and he's not answering his phone, probably buried in some calculation or something, I know what he's like. But he said they want this report bound today.'

Mary grabbed the opportunity. 'Is he the guy with the b-big scar?'

'No, that's Gabriel, the IT manager. Marcus has red hair and a beard.'

'Oh yes, I remember,' said Mary innocently and set out for the third floor, thinking, Gabriel! My guardian angel, Gabriel!

9

Gabriel considered his options for a few hours before he decided what would be his best course of action. The incident in the lift had demonstrated that the effect of him confronting those guys in the parking building had not lasted. And not only that, but the one who worked at Tidewell's had been talking to at least one other who also worked there. That he must do something to stop the harassment of Mary was clear, and after thinking about it he decided to call her brother John, whom he hadn't seen for years. The moment she had mentioned six brothers he had known who she was.

'Hi,' he said briefly when John took his call that evening. 'It's Gab from the uni rugby team. Have you got time to talk?'

'Yeah, not a problem. It's a very long time since I saw you last, but good to hear from you. We should try to have some kind of reunion of the team sometime - we used to have a lot of fun after the matches, didn't we?'

'I'm back in our old hometown now, working as the IT manager for a research company. Dinner would be nice, but for now I've got something urgent you can help with. You won't know this, but the company I work for is the one where Mary got a job a few weeks ago, and there's something nasty going on which needs sorting out. Well, it needs to be stopped. She's being seriously harassed by a group of guys, a bit like stalking and widely known. They're having bets online about it.'

John's voice took on a hard edge. 'What exactly are they doing?'

Gabriel sighed. 'One of those sick things that some guys get up to now, you know – having bets on who can get a particular girl into bed first and proving it by taking sneaky videos. And then sharing the videos online. I first heard about it only recently. I have a space reserved in the parking building that links up with ours. I was coming down the ramp instead of using the stairs when I heard them laughing. They couldn't see me, so I stopped and listened for a few minutes, just to get to grip on what the hell they were talking about.'

'Fucking creeps!' said John. 'Not what she needs at all, this isn't good! What did you do?'

'I walked right up to them before they noticed me and gave them one hell of a lecture and told them it had to stop right away, or else.'

'I know you could probably mash them if you wanted to, but it's still going on, is it?'

'I'm sure it is. Mary knows, she told me someone had warned her about them. She clearly doesn't know how to deal with it, and she finds it unsettling. Well, there's probably not much she can do. I can't remember her precise words, but what she meant was that it makes her feel like she's prey. And she's right, that's precisely how it is, they're predators and she's the prey.'

'OK, obviously we must deal with it. Any suggestions?'

Gabriel smiled to himself. 'Remember when we were at uni and you took off for a couple of days and missed that semi-final game we lost, and we all gave you hell about it? You told me where you'd been and showed me the video, the event that became know all over campus as the Lintott line-up once the video got circulated? If a couple of your brothers could do something a bit like that, very publicly, it might stop these creeps.'

There was a long pause at the other end, then John spoke decisively. 'Yeah, we can. We're all getting together for my dad's seventy-fifth birthday the weekend after next. I'll make sure we all get there on the Friday afternoon. I'll have to tell the others to let Mary know we'll be there by Friday evening and that we've ordered pizza to be delivered for dinner, so she doesn't worry about the food situation.'

'And you'll do a line-up somewhere public, preferably where those guys will hear about it?'

'Of course, that's the whole point. Is your reception area on the ground floor? I know where Tidewell's is, and I assume the whole building is yours, but do we have to use a lift to get to reception? It's on the ground floor? Good! I think if the six of us turn up, walk up to the building in formation and approach the reception desk, we could command a bit of attention.' He chuckled. 'I think I can visualise what your building looks like - it's set back from the street with a forecourt in front, isn't it? So we could form the line outside, perhaps from the edge of the sidewalk and go from there. Double doors or a single door?'

'Big twin glass doors, automatic. Both slide open when you approach.' Gabriel was laughing now. 'Christ! I can see it as we speak. You lot lining up right back at the street and walking towards the doors – just like when you went to Mary's high school when she was being bullied. Fantastic! How old was she then?'

John laughed too. 'God, that was so great, I'll never forget that day. She had just turned thirteen and started high school. She was being bullied because of her stammer, and some days she was so upset she refused to go to school. So we planned it, all got together from wherever we were at that stage and walked across the school yard in a dead straight line, shoulder to shoulder. The youngest of us had left school the year before Mopsy started. We stopped and waited until all the kids noticed us, and Mopsy saw us and came over, very, very slowly, so William who was in the centre of the line, motioned her closer. She stopped right in front of him, and we closed into a circle with her in the middle.'

'I remember the video – it was an amazing sight.'

'You've never seen a school yard at a major high school so full of totally silent kids. Not a sound and nobody moved, it was like a freeze frame image. It gave me goose bumps. We just stood there in our circle quietly talking and asked her if she wanted to point out any tormentors in particular, but she said no. She thought us being there would be enough, but she wanted us to straighten out the line again and kind of scan the yard – all of us, slowly, from one side to the other, so that's what we did, if you remember. Made sure every single kid there knew we had looked straight at them, or that's what they thought.' He laughed, delighted with his little sister. 'That video clip spread like wildfire. And then we left, and we obeyed her instructions not to kiss her or hug her, which is what we normally do. She's such a little planner!'

'I remember the video spreading on campus after you'd shown it to me, and I never thought of it at the time, but how did you get it? Who filmed it?'

John laughed again, revelling in the story from ten years earlier. 'Just luck! We saw a girl outside the gates when we got there – she looked like a senior coming in at lunchtime for some reason, so William unlocked his phone and opened the camera and handed it to her. He said "Walk in now and go and stand on the top step outside the main doors and be ready to film us. Keep the camera going until we leave, then you come out to the street and give me the phone back and I'll give you twenty bucks." And that's what she did, she had a perfect vantage point standing five steps higher than everyone else.'

'It was an amazing sight,' said Gabriel, remembering how impressed he had been when he saw the video, which was the first time he had realised that John had five brothers. 'Six tall guys - all with that famous hair.'

'So how did you know Mary's my sister? Did she tell

you, or was it the hair?' John laughed. 'That genetic link from dad is so strong, and now my daughter has it too, she looks just like Mopsy, sorry, I mean Mary. Dad's mother was from southern Italy.'

'She mentioned six brothers, so in combination with the hair it was quite clear. Text me when you gather outside next Friday, will you? I wouldn't want to miss this for anything.'

After briefly telling John about the incident in the lift, Gabrial ended the call and congratulated himself on having avoided any mention of being locked in a dark room with Mary or what had followed. He poured a glass of wine and went back to his chair, his mind constructing images of what the scene in the Tidewell reception might turn into; he smiled.

'Hi Mopsy,' said John when Mary took a call on her phone that night. 'Listen, Sylvia and I were talking in the car on the way home from James's birthday and we both think that for dad's big birthday next week we should try to get there on the Friday afternoon or evening, at least at many of us as can manage it. You know the chaos that always breaks out when we arrive in dribs and drabs on a Saturday, and then on the Sunday we break up in stages. It makes it really hard to get to talk individually to everyone. What do you think?'

'That's a great idea!' Mary had never thought of this because she was the one who was always there and hadn't realised that for some it got fragmented. 'And we always have the beds made up as soon as all the sheets are washed, so there's nothing that needs doing, and we can have a casual meal at home on the Friday night.'

'No, that makes it far too much work for you! Let's have a giant take-out dinner of some kind that all of us can eat. You have enough to do and it's a workday. How about Chinese? Sylvia said just now that after your speech at James's birthday dinner she knows what the food problems are, so we can just order it beforehand, and nobody needs to do anything in particular. Just get dad to buy a couple of extra loaves of bread for toast for Saturday morning and lots of milk, and we'll be fine.'

Let's see how many can get Friday afternoon off to get here, thought Mary when she put the phone down. But even half the boys arriving early would be lovely, and dad would like a bit more time with us all together, seeing it's his special birthday weekend.

10

When Mary arrived at the French Bistro on Saturday afternoon, Maylene and Ava were already at the table she had reserved, their favourite table in the round alcove.

'You're the only one who remembers to call them and ask for this table to be reserved,' said Maylene. 'I don't know how you got given the boring job of always being more organised than the rest of us. I hope you know we appreciate it, hapless, slapdash girls that we are.'

'I'll expect you t-to show your appreciation on my b-birthday. And this alcove's perfect for f-four, isn't it? A nearly closed circle, so we c-can just fit on the banquette and all see each other. I love it – it's like a l-little secret room.'

Andrea, who had turned up in time to hear this exchange, slid into the semicircular seat where she aways sat beside Mary, and said, 'She's the queen of logistics, isn't she? Look at all those amazing events she orchestrates for the Lintott tribe. And several times a year, too. Makes my efforts to help mum with preparations for Christmas seem ridiculous.'

But suddenly her hand reached out and tapped Mary's thigh under the table and following her glance Mary saw Greg approaching. She made a lightning fast decision and whispered, 'Don't say *anything*!' to Andrea and kept her face neutral.

'Mary, can we please have a chat - in private?' Greg stopped beside their table, looking as impossibly handsome as ever and very serious.

'Why?'

'I want to apologise,' he said, and his eyes flicked to the others. 'In private, so I can explain.'

'No.' She was pleased that her voice didn't reveal how angry she was.

'Please, just a few minutes of your time, I promise.' This was a man who was not used to pleading, he was clearly struggling to sound composed instead of irritated.

'There *is* n-no excuse or explanation for sneakily p-putting a t-tracking app on m-my phone. Just go away!'

Dismissively Mary turned towards Andrea and didn't see Greg hesitating for a moment before he walked away to the far end of the room.

Wide-eyed Maylene stared after Greg, then at Mary. 'Did he really put a tracking app on your phone?'

'He d-did. And he hid it, so I c-couldn't see it in my app folder, the sneaky b-bastard. I can see that Andrea is d-dying to tell you. I'm over it!'

Andrea scowled in Greg's direction. 'I was here when he chatted her up, he was right over there, close to where he is now, when she came out of the toilets. And after a few minutes I saw her hand her phone to him, but it was a ploy - he didn't just enter his number, he also planted that tracker thing.' She told them the saga which Mary had texted her after she had coffee with Greg, including how she took photos of both Greg and of the woman who had taken pictures of her.

When she reached the end and after indignant exclamations of outrage, Ava said decisively. 'You guys stay here. I'm going to order some bar snacks.'

She got up, all six foot two of her, dressed in jeans and a man's white shirt and stalked on long legs across the floor like a warrior on a mission.

'Watch her!' said Andrea. 'She's up to something. I know that walk and that dangerous look. I hope she doesn't use her kick boxing skills and knocks him out in public.'

Greg, who was now sitting at the bar talking to the girl beside him, had his back turned and literally jumped when Ava stopped right behind him and said something. It took no time at all, a minute later Ava turned to the barman, Greg got off his stool and headed for the door not looking at anyone and disappeared.

Looking calm and serious as usual Ava returned and slid into her seat. 'I've ordered tapas for us all and another beer for me. Are you guys OK for drinks?'

'What did you say to him?' Maylene looked like a child with a surprise present in front of her, avid to hear the details. 'You were only there a minute and then he left!'

Ava grinned. 'First I told the girl he was talking to that I'm a police officer and she'd better be careful, because he puts tracking apps on girls' phones, and then I turned to look him in the eye and said, "You're a top class shit, mate. I'm now going to inform the staff here what you get up to, so maybe you'd better stay away from this place from now on". That's all.'

She paused and added regretfully, 'I really wanted to knock him down, so I could watch him writhing in pain on the floor, but then I'd lose my job, and Mary would have been embarrassed, so I didn't.'

They collapsed in laughter, and after a few moments Mary wiped tears from her eyes and was just about to say something when a man appeared at their table.

'I'm Russell, the manager,' he said. 'Did one of you tell the bar staff that someone had put a tracking app on her phone just now?'

'I did, but not on my phone, and it didn't happen just now,' said Ava and got up again. 'My name's Ava Whitlock, I'm a police officer. He put it on my friend Mary's phone a while ago, here in this bar, pretended he was only putting his number in. And he hid it, so it didn't show in her apps list.' She turned to Mary. 'Can you pull up those pictures of him and that woman, so this guy can see what he looks like?'

She waited until Mary handed over her phone and turned back to the bar manager with it held out for him to see. 'This is the one, his name is Greg somebody. I reckon you should print it and put it up in the women's toilets with a warning. And black-list him. He's a menace!'

Russell pulled up a chair from a neighbouring table and sat down. 'I hope you don't mind, but I'd like to have the full story. I won't tell anyone else, but I'd like to know how this happened, how you got photos of those two. I've never noticed that guy before, but as you say, a printout of this guy would be good. Maybe have one in the ladies' restroom and one beside the cash register, so we can tell him to get out if he turns up again.'

Mary had to make a fast decision about how much to tell him and sat thinking for a moment while they all waited. But perhaps the biggest impact would be to tell him about the abduction which was the reason this had happened. It would make her stammer worse than ever, but it would tell him that he needed to take Greg's devious attempt to gain her confidence seriously.

'It's about s-something that happened when I was a child,' she said. 'Something very t-traumatic, b-but you n-need to know, I think. It explains what he was after and how d-devious he is. I was abducted when I was three and a half and he was hoping to use m-me to earn m-money on YouTube. My s-stammer is one of the l-lasting effects of what happened to m-me.'

He listened with his eyes locked on hers until she finished with an internal sigh of relief. Talking to a complete stranger was always exhausting, but it had worked. Russell got up and said with obvious sincerity, 'I knew about the abduction, of course. I was at high school at the time, and I'm really sorry this happened to you at our place. Please email that photo to us – you'll find the email address on the website, and I'll print it and make sure our staff have a good look at it. I'm going to put in a bar tab credit in our system in your name, for you girls to use, because I hope you will come back! I'm sure that scumbag won't have the nerve to come here again.'

'Awesome!' exclaimed Maylene when he had gone. 'Ava, you're a star, you really are! Watching you stride across the floor like an avenging angel, magnificent! The blue team, as you call them, is lucky to have you.'

Two hours later they parted outside, Ava and Maylene in one direction and Andrea and Mary going the opposite way. 'You were so brave telling him a bit about the abduction,' said Andrea as they waited for the bus in a blustery wind that whipped Mary's black curls over her face. 'I thought it might be a bit much, but I was ready to take over if need be.'

Mary held her hair back with one hand and put the other on Andrea's arm. 'Thank you, b-but I'm OK talking about it. It's only when someone t-tries to pry into the p-potential sexual part that I choke and can't continue. It's n-not that he did anything to me, as you know, it's the f-feeling that they expect something shocking, the l-look on their faces. A b-bit sick making.'

Andrea's expression alerted her, and she realised that they had never talked about the two incidents when this had happened. 'D-don't panic! It's only happened twice, men b-both times.'

'Bloody vultures,' said Andrea, scowling ferociously. 'Next time you should call Ava – tell her to come along and scare them to death.'

They grinned at each other and changed the subject, and Mary was glad that she hadn't been asked who the other man was, who'd pried about the abduction, because it was someone Andrea knew, she was friends with both him and his sister. No point in ruining her friendship with him, thought Mary, and got her bus card out. He'd probably realised how awful those questions were and learned something by her walking off and leaving him standing there with her half eaten taco.

That night she called Richard and heard someone saying something in the background when he took the call. 'Have you got company? I can call another time, it's nothing urgent.'

'No, it's fine. I've got a friend here to watch the test match, but it doesn't start for half an hour. What's up?'

'You know that tracking app you helped me with? I was in the bistro for a late afternoon catchup with some friends and that guy was there, he came up to our table and asked to talk to me in private. To apologise and explain! As if any explanation would help. But I said no.'

'Good on you! That kind of creep is best ignored, I think. Did he leave you alone after that?'

Mary smiled to herself. 'When I told him I wouldn't talk to him I mentioned the tracker and he left - went back to the bar and sat down beside a woman, and the others who were with me wanted to know what the tracker was about, so I got Andrea to tell the story. I really couldn't be bothered,' She laughed quietly. 'But this is the best bit. Ava was with us, you remember her, don't you? The tall girl who's in the police now.'

Richard chuckled. 'She'd be hard to forget, that girl. You probably don't know this, but she and her dad used to come to that boxing gym I belonged to. She'd only have been ten or so at the time and she was a great little fighter. So she's joined the police, has she? She'll be an asset in that kind of job.'

'She's an asset to me, too,' said Mary. 'Listen to this! When Andrea had told them what it was about, Ava got up and stalked across the floor like some warrior on a mission. You have to try to picture this if you haven't seen her since she was ten. She's about your height now, dresses like a man and nearly always wears boots, and she's got something called a brown belt in kickboxing, which I gather means she could kick someone to death if she wanted to. So she went up behind Greg and told him he's a shit, and then she warned the woman he was talking to that he puts trackers on women's phones – and *then* she told the bar staff the same. And he got off his stool and walked right out the door and disappeared!'

'Great stuff! Tell Ava hi from me next time you see her, and let's hope that guy stays away from your favourite bistro.'

Mary told him the rest of the story and when she put the phone down, she felt a new level of calm about the Greg saga in her mind. Having told Richard the whole thing had helped put it in perspective, made it an event that took place in the past, and she knew she could disregard it now and not dwell on it.

11

Mary was using the new stick vacuum cleaner in the old living room and hadn't heard the doorbell, so when Andrea suddenly appeared beside her she jumped in surprise. She lifted the headphones off her head and turned the cleaner off. 'God, you g-gave me a fright!'

Andrea was in her gym gear, so she must have come straight from her early Saturday morning session as a part-time personal trainer at the fancy women's gym in Norfolk Street, the one John called the body factory.

'I rang the bell and knocked and then I thought I heard something, so I walked around to the back, and I could hear the cleaner through the open kitchen door. It's quite noisy, isn't it? Is it new?'

'Brand new – dad b-bought it yesterday and you're right, the noise is hideous. It has a k-kind of high-pitched tone to it that's really p-painful, so I was wearing headphones to make it tolerable. I haven't the heart to t-tell him how awful it is.'

'Will he ever use it?'

'Oh, he will – he often cleans or dusts, but he p-probably won't hear that high n-note. You know how older p-people can't hear the cicadas? Same thing, I think. He'll just think I'm listening to m-music while I c-clean the floors. Do you want a c-coffee?'

It was perfectly clear that Andrea had come with a purpose in mind. Popping in unannounced was unusual for her, and Mary couldn't remember a single impromptu visit this early in the day since they were children. Vaguely worried, she leaned the vacuum cleaner against the back of an armchair and led the way to the kitchen, hoping Andrea's ex-partner hadn't caused problems again. As Andrea had said last time he sent her a rude text message, 'He's the one who left me for someone else, but if I go out with someone and he hears about it he thinks he can start criticising again. Such a control freak!'

'Dad's p-playing golf this morning and you've c-come straight from the gym.' Mary laughed. 'All I've d-done is get dressed and a bit of housework.'

Andrea pulled out a chair at the kitchen table and watched Mary make two mugs of coffee. 'Come on! T-tell me what's wrong,' said Mary over her shoulder and reached for the biscuit packet in the pantry. 'Something's on your m-mind, it's l-like an air current around you – what is it?'

'Someone at the gym told me there's a lot of chat on social media about us – you know, the time when Ava went up to that guy Greg and told him to leave the bistro. And there's a photo of her standing beside him and another one of him walking out. I just thought I should warn you – it's being shared a lot. My mum saw it and told me last night, and then a girl mentioned it at the gym this morning. She knows his full name.'

'Oh, that thing! D-don't worry, it's been d-doing the rounds for ages. Henry t-told me about it not long after it happened, he saw it first on Instagram, I think.'

'I didn't want you to worry about it. The image I saw on Facebook was taken from the diagonal corner from where we were, so it showed Ava standing beside Greg and us in the background on the other side of the room.'

Mary smiled to reassure Andrea. 'It's fine! But thanks f-for worrying about me. It's p-probably the same photos Henry saw. Are there lots of c-comments now?'

'Dozens! I read them all and nobody's mentioned his surname, or not yet anyway, but his face is clearly visible in the second shot when he gets off his stool and heads for the door, so it's only a question of time. And one person, who commented, posted a shot she had taken of the bar manager sitting at our table, and she must have heard what he said when he first came to talk to us. Remember how he asked which one of us had had a tracking app sneakily put on a phone? She quoted that in her comment, verbatim. She's either got fantastic hearing, or she was recording our conversation.'

Why had Andrea worried how she would take this news? Mary was puzzled, but Andrea had been protective of her ever since she had been Mary's escort to and from school when they were children.

'I really don't c-care even if I'm named in the c-comments sometime in the f-future.' Mary pushed the biscuit packet toward Andrea. 'Try one of these, they're g-gorgeous. Dad discovered them the other d-day. But I can't see there's anything f-for me to be concerned about ... I've done nothing wrong. And Greg d-deserves to be shamed, if not n-named. But why would that woman have r-recorded the chat we had with the b-bar manager?'

Andrea laughed and held up her hand, counting things off on her fingers. 'I thought about this on the way here and here's my theory . First she watched Ava doing her high focus march across the floor – she's a very noticeable girl, our Ava. Then she watched her talking to Greg and that girl he sat next to and then talking to the bartender. Then she either filmed us as Ava returned or just watched us. So when the bar manager turned up and sat down she took a photo, then she started filming, and when she watched what she had filmed she could probably turn up the volume and hear what he said, that first bit when he asked what had happened.' She laughed again. 'I've run out of fingers, but I think that covers it.'

Mary considered this scenario, laid out like a timeline and nodded. 'You're right, and I c-can imagine exactly where she m-must have been sitting, too. Not that I noticed at the t-time, but it can't have happened any other way.'

'*But*,' said Andrea significantly and pointed her biscuit at Mary, 'that's not all. There's also an article on one of the major newspaper websites about it, it went up last night. This girl at the gym mentioned that it had appeared yesterday, so I checked it out before I came over. It's a very good article, mostly about this kind of nastiness in general, and it doesn't name him, but it has screenshots of the crucial social media posts and some of the comments. Who would have thought it would get so much traction?'

They were still sitting there with a second cup of coffee and another biscuit each when Archie walked in the back door. 'Andrea, hi, how nice to see you! It's pouring down out west, so we couldn't continue playing. And I think those clouds followed me across town, it's just about to start raining here too.'

Mary quickly tried to imagine how she could prevent Andrea telling her father anything that would lead him to hear the full Greg saga, which she had never mentioned and never would. And just as she opened her mouth to ask him if he wanted a coffee Andrea said calmly, 'I've just updated Mary on the latest about that shit Greg, who's now been thoroughly exposed in social media and even in the press! I thought she might worry, but she seems quite pleased.'

Mary held her breath. What would he ask and how much should she tell him? But no, there was no need to worry. Her father said calmly, 'Excellent, he deserves to be exposed. Henry told me the whole story a little while ago and I've been hoping something more than just being blacklisted at that bistro would come of it.' He turned to Mary and grinned. 'I can see you're surprised, Mopsy, but you know that if one of your brothers knows something relating to you, odds are we'll all know within hours or at least days.'

Mary rolled her eyes, and Andrea laughed. 'I'd be very happy to trade my privacy for brothers and a father like yours. You don't know how lucky you are.'

'Oh, I d-do know – I just p-pretend that I mind. It's like having a whole t-troop of bodyguards.'

12

When Maylene texted and asked Mary to call when she had five or ten minutes to talk, she was mystified. She tried to imagine what this could mean, because the last couple of times they had met, Maylene had seemed a little subdued and not quite like her usual cheerful self. Slightly worried she replied, "call me in five minutes" and went to sit on the terrace in the sun. She rolled her sleeves up and thought how wonderful it felt with sunlight on her skin after the first half of spring this year which had sometimes felt more like winter.

'Hi,' said Maylene a few minutes later. 'Listen, this is the weirdest thing I've ever had to ask anyone, totally embarrassing, but you remember I told you my mother's moving out of her big flat into a little one? Since she and dad split up she's not handled money well, and she got herself into a mess. So dad, being the kind man he is, said he'd pay the back rent owing on her current flat, and he's found her a smaller one at half the cost. But now she wants you to come and talk through things with her.'

Mary laughed in disbelief. 'Really? What on earth d-does she want my advice on? Aren't your dad and you the b-best people to advise her?'

'You know how I sometimes say quite casually that my mum's place is a real mess? Well, that's not quite true. The truth is that she's a hoarder, the place is a disaster, chock full of stuff she buys in charity shops or online. And it's mostly things she doesn't need and never uses, but it explains why she's in a financial mess. So it's got to be sorted out before she moves, and she's totally rejected any input from the family.'

'OK, b-but I still don't understand why she's asking f-for me,' said Mary slowly and ran her hand up though her hair to lift if off the back of her neck. 'I think you'll have t-to explain. I would have thought I'd be t-totally unsuited to the t-task and I haven't seen her f-face to face for years and I have no idea what she needs to k-keep.'

Maylene laughed, but not as if she was enjoying anything. 'She needs *none* of that junk, that's the problem. She buys something she has no use for, puts it down just anywhere and then it gets buried under more purchases – it's a disaster zone covered in dust. So when I asked her to suggest someone to help her make decisions, seeing I was obviously not the right person, I thought she'd say her sister, but she said straight off that she wanted you.'

'D-do you know why?'

'Well, I asked her that and she said you have a reputation for being super organised and decisive and she'd heard stories about how you've organised that whole clan of yours for celebrations and Christmas and whatever from when you were in your mid-teens. And once she'd said that I kind of had to agree, of course. And you could probably handle her, but it's a ghastly task to ask of anyone who's not used to her.'

'Do you think we c-could do it in stages? I m-mean, if it's real hands-on help she n-needs.' Mary was thinking of a TV series she'd watched some years ago, where two women went into messy houses and sorted things out. In her mind's eye she imagined a dumpster sitting outside being gradually filled with junk, other things going back to charity shops or to the auction rooms. Probably a giant task that might involve tears and tantrums from Mrs Wong, who was known to all Maylene's friends as someone who was temperamental and often contrary. She remembered Maylene telling her of the day her father decided to move out, when he could no longer deal with it, and how her mother had run after the car for a whole block screaming abuse at him.

'I think it would be best to just go and talk to her first,' said Maylene. 'Just tell her very firmly that she can't take it all and that some hard decisions have to be made. I tried and got told to be quiet if I had nothing better to say. Dad tried and was told to butt out, and Liam flatly refuses to even try. You probably don't know this, but the reason he moved out when he turned sixteen wasn't that living with our aunt and uncle meant he was closer to the Polytech, it was the mess. He's super tidy, nearly obsessively so, and he couldn't stand it – he used to say it gave him a rash just looking at it. And that was before it turned into the total chaos it is now.'

Mary knew she had no choice. This family needed help, and if they thought she could provide it, she must at least try. 'We've g-got my father's b-big birthday party next weekend, and I can't do much until that's over, but how about I g-go over one day after work and just have a chat? When is she m-moving?'

'Oh, not until just before Christmas when the new flat becomes vacant. We just thought maybe starting now would be a good idea because it's not a job that will be done in one day.'

'M-maybe we can stage it, so she gets used to it a bit at a t-time, and ramp it up a bit more each time, like more and faster d-decisions, more radical advice. What do you think?'

Maylene said on a sob, 'Oh God, you're just the best! You can't imagine how worried I've been about asking you. Thank you! I'll be in touch.'

Mary sat slightly stunned with the phone in her hand and tried to picture how this could possibly work. A stubborn, difficult woman who had already rejected everyone's offers to help, a woman she had not talked to for years and only met a few times in her life. They had nothing in common and no shared interests apart from Maylene, so it was hard to imagine what use she could be.

Later that day a vague idea grew in her mind that her father had mentioned some time ago that he had known

Mrs Wong in the past, though she couldn't remember the context.

'Hey, dad,' she said when he returned from visiting a friend in hospital. 'I'm just about to make a coffee to take outside, it's gorgeous out on the terrace, no wind at all today. I see you bought some of those coconut macaroons so we could open those.'

'I'd love a coffee, but I want to wash my hands first. I can't stand that alcohol based disinfectant they have in the hospital, it stinks forever.'

By the time her father came back from the bathroom the coffee was made. 'You take your cup and the biscuits,' said Mary, 'and I'll take my cup and the phone. And tell me, why did you use that sanitizer if you dislike the smell of it?'

'I had to. At the moment Andrew is in an isolation ward for a week because his immune system has dropped to rock bottom after the last chemotherapy session for some reason and visitors have to be careful. He's in a room with positive air pressure, so no bugs get in - I had to wear a mask too.'

They sat side by side looking out over the enormous expanse of the back garden where the only things other than grass were four fruit trees, which most springs were covered in blossoms, one after the other as if planned by nature. This was where impromptu games of cricket were played at any time of the day when her brothers came home for visits, and where Mary had played games of chase with her brothers when she was little, screaming with nearly real fear when they just missed catching her.

'Do you remember how the boys used to chase me in that game they invented? And I sometimes got really scared they'd grab me, even though I knew it was a game? I must have been fast – I didn't often get caught.'

Her father turned and watched her face for a long moment. 'You didn't realise they did that on purpose? They *let* you just get away practically all the time, it was part of what they called the resilience training.'

Mary stared at him, not sure if she understood what he was saying. 'Resilience training? Was that game some kind of training for me?'

'Listen,' said her dad calmly. 'Don't get upset now, but I never thought to mention it, and I thought you'd worked it out years ago, anyway. After the abduction, when you were terrified of everyone apart from us here at home, the boys thought they'd bolster your confidence by making you feel you had options, like you could scream very loudly, like in that scream-if-I-scare-you game, and the chase game, to get you used to reacting fast and running away.'

Mary's eyes flooded with tears. How could she not have understood that there was a purpose behind those games? All these years she had thought it was just games with no purpose other than to have fun with her.

'Aren't they wonderful? God, how I love those boys for always taking care of me! And I never realised, you know. I just thought I was faster than them, but not I think of it, of course, they could have caught me easily every time. Do you think the training games worked?'

'No, not at all,' said her dad comfortably. 'But it didn't matter, did it? They felt they were being constructive and helping you cope, so it made them feel better, and in the meantime you all had noisy fun out here, so it was a win-win situation.'

They sat in silence for a few minutes, both thinking back to the year and half between the abduction and when she started school. The eighteen months when they had all helped her readjust and regain her confidence with the world at large. She knew they had been worried that she would be traumatised for the rest of her life, but apart from her stammering with anyone not part of the family, they had managed to revive her fearless, bossy spirit.

To change the subject she asked the question she had thought of earlier. 'Did you tell me once that you know Mrs Wong, Maylene's mother?'

'Many years ago I did, but I haven't seen her for ages. I used to have a chat to her sometimes when she worked in the café out at the golf club, but she hasn't been there for a long time. Why?'

When he heard about the hoarding problem he laughed out loud. 'If anyone could sort her out it would be you, Mopsy. Just have a go and see what it leads to. And Maylene will be grateful even if it doesn't work - at least you tried,'

13

At twenty to three on the Friday the week after his phone call to John, Gabriel received a text that read: "We're ready to line up in a couple of minutes, have your phone ready to film, preferably from inside reception."

He raced down the fire stairs rather than take the lift; no way was he going to risk missing this. Gretchen looked strangely at him when he went to stand level with her desk but right over to one side beside one of the huge potted plants. With his phone in his hand he waited only for a minute, and then, there they were, right back at the edge of the sidewalk, and he nearly laughed at the sight. They were all dressed in black, casual clothes but black from top to toe. Shoulder to shoulder they walked towards the big glass doors while Gabriel filmed them. Beside him he heard Gretchen's gasp of surprise and then her alarmed voice saying something, but he was too concentrated on what was happening in front of his eyes to pay attention. The Lintott line-up advanced very, very slowly until the big doors slid aside and they could proceed into the huge foyer where they stopped halfway to the reception desk.

Gabriel turned slightly to capture Gretchen's stunned face as she scanned the line of men in front of her from left to right, then he took a few steps back to stand behind the giant plants in the corner, out of sight by someone coming down either via the lift or the stairs, but he never stopped filming for a moment. The one he assumed was William, the oldest Lintott brother, spoke calmly, very serious. 'Can you please ask Mary Lintott to come down?'

Her voice a bit shaky, Gretchen asked, 'Why? What are you going to do to her?'

'Nothing, she's our sister and we want to see her. We would never harm her, never. First get Mary down here and then call your CEO and ask him to come down, too.'

'OK.' Gretchen made a phone call, briefly telling someone that Mary had visitors waiting in reception, and then one to someone called Rebecca asking that Mr Ford came down. They all waited in silence until the lift doors opened, and Gabriel moved his angle to take in Mary as she emerged laughing. 'Oh, my God, you lot!'

William beckoned. 'Come here, you know the drill – remember the school yard?'

She walked across slowly across the foyer until she was just in front of him and turned, saying quietly over her shoulder, 'What now?'

'Now we wait.' And so they did. They stood there, tall and black haired, silent and impressive, not looking at each other, and Mary stood unmoving in front of William until the CEO appeared beside Gretchen's desk.

'Good afternoon!' said William. 'We are Mary's brothers and, as on another occasion when she was bullied or harassed, we have come to show that she's not alone, we stand behind her at all times. Just so the group of guys, who are planning to seriously abuse her, can see she's not without protection.'

Very briefly they closed a circle around Mary, who disappeared completely from view behind their tall bodies, then they broke the formation and William walked calmly over to Stuart and held out his hand. 'William Lintott,' he said, as if nothing unusual had taken place. 'You must be Stuart Ford, I recognise you from the Tidewell website. Is there somewhere we can have a quick chat? Just you and me, I mean, not the whole lot of us.'

Suddenly applause and loud voices erupted from the mezzanine gallery, and Gabriel raised his phone: the gallery above reception was crowded, phones held up in nearly every pair of hands. Stuart and William disappeared into the lift, probably heading for Stuart's office, and Gabriel turned his phone off. Gretchen found her voice and asked the remaining five Lintott brothers if they would like to sit down in the staff canteen and have a coffee while they waited, but they politely declined.

'We'll borrow Mary for a few minutes,' said John coolly, put his arm over Mary's shoulders and led the way outside.

Those on the mezzanine floor had dispersed, Gabriel walked away down the corridor on the far side of reception and returned by a circuitous route to his office, and Gretchen was suddenly alone in the vast marble foyer, still stunned.

The rest of the afternoon became the most unproductive couple of hours the company had ever experienced. People gathered in small groups showing each other photos and videos on their phones, the staff cafeteria was busy with a constantly changing population coming for coffee and to show others their phone footage. Nobody worked as usual apart from a couple of lab technicians, who simply couldn't leave what they were doing and only heard about the event at the end of the day. By then the video Gabriel had emailed to John was already on Facebook and Instagram and being shared by hundreds, and so where other videos from those who had watched the spectacle from the gallery.

'My God!' exclaimed Gretchen half an hour later, when William had left and Mary came back inside. 'Talk about the men in black! Aren't you a lucky girl to have those staunch brothers looking out for you?'

Mary smiled. 'I know, they're amazing, they've b-been like this all my l-life. They're all so much older than me and they've been my p-protectors since the day I was b-born.'

'Well, now you're back inside I'll lock the doors. Stuart said we're not admitting any more visitors today and we can all relax and have coffee or whatever.'

'Is he really n-not angry? William said he wasn't, b-but he might be angry with m-me.' The thought that this might not end well for her relationship with management had been on her mind since John walked her out of the building, but Gretchen just laughed. 'Oh no, not at all. He and you brother had that short meeting, and then they came down and shook hands before your brother left. They were all smiles, don't worry!'

14

Later that afternoon Mary walked up the street from the bus stop and smiled at the sight of the driveway with four cars parked in pairs, which made perfect sense. Only two of her brothers would have flown in, and they had obviously been picked up by the others to go and do their thing at Tidewell's. Before she was even on the path to the front door she heard voices and laughter from the back garden and the *thwack!* of a wooden bat hitting a ball. A perfectly normal gathering of the clan, the way it always happened if it was warm and light enough when they arrived, so instead of going in through the front door she walked around the house and stopped by the corner. Two teams of three bothers playing cricket on the big lawn with two children taking part, and a little crowd watching from the deck with mugs of coffee or cans of beer in their hands. She noticed that today Yolanta was once again talking to Sylvia, probably about books again, and hoped this new relationship of James's would last longer than the last two.

Without having been noticed, she retreated to the front door and let herself in. If they saw her now this lovely scene in the garden would get interrupted and possibly not re-started, as her brothers hugged her and everyone started discussing the line-up. So she got out of her work clothes and put on shorts and a T-shirt and spent half an hour in the kitchen setting out piles of plates and glasses on the table, added the roll of kitchen paper for sticky hands, and checked the fridge for beer and wine until everything was ready for the Chinese food delivery that John and Sylvia had promised to organise. She was standing there surveying the kitchen bench and the table, when John turned up behind her and put his arms around her lifting her off her feet as he always did, even today when he had seen her only a few hours ago.

'Mopsy! I didn't know you'd got home yet. Are you hiding?' He kissed the top of her head, put her down and turned her around. 'What happened after we left?'

'Oh, total chaos for the rest of the afternoon, you have no idea! The CEO told Gretchen, that's the receptionist, to lock the doors, and everyone spent the last hour and a half drinking coffee and sharing their photos and videos. I bet the whole thing's on every social media site you can think of by now.'

'Did you see the video that shows us right from the start when we lined up at the edge of the forecourt? It's great – it even takes in the stunned face of the receptionist and then you coming out of the lift laughing, the whole thing.'

Her smile faded, and she looked hard at him, intent on getting to the bottom of this mysterious event. 'So, who was it? He or she must have stood behind that huge plant, you can see the leaves when they turned the phone up to film the mezzanine floor.'

'I'm sworn to silence, so I can't tell you, sorry!' John tried to look innocent, but she outstared him in silence.

'OK,' he said finally when he realised she was not going to let this go. 'Someone gave me a hint, and I organised the rest of the boys, and told you a little white lie about why we would all arrive today.' He held up his hand when she opened her mouth to say something. 'Hang on, just let me finish, please. There is a little bonus in this deceit, you know. Everyone's already agreeing that coming today was a great idea because we actually get a chance to do things together. Like playing cricket and just hanging out talking here at home, much less rushed than normal when we just have part of Saturday and a bit on Sunday morning, more like when we get together at Christmas.'

'Oh, it's lovely, I totally agree,' said Mary, 'and particularly for dad, but I'd still love to know who told you, and *particularly* how that person knew to contact you. I've been thinking about it ever since you left. I know you said it was a secret when we chatted outside while William was with the CEO, but I'd really like to know. I think it must have been the same person, who knew to be there in the foyer ready to film it right from the very start. So, you warned whoever it was to come down with his phone?'

'Sorry, Mopsy! I promised not to tell.' John grinned at her frustrated expression. 'I know you nearly always get what you want from me, but not this time.'

She could tell he meant it, so she smiled, got up on

tiptoes to kiss his cheek and picked up a beer before she followed him outside to say hi to everyone else. The game was over, everyone wanted to hear how surprised she had been at the appearance of her brothers that afternoon and insisted on showing her the various videos they had found on social media.

By the time the Chinese food had been picked up by Henry and John and set out in the kitchen, everyone seemed to be starving, and a line quickly formed to walk around the table and fill their plates. Mary and Henry were waiting for their turn, last in the line.

'What a great idea those little flags saying gluten free and seafood free are,' said Mary. 'I've never seen them before. I'll keep them for future use. Thank God, we don't have anyone who's allergic to peanuts or things would become really complicated. Have the others signed the special birthday card you got somebody to make?'

Henry laughed. 'I thought we could all sign it at the dinner after I give it to dad. I'd like him to see it before anyone else, it's very special. My new boyfriend designed it and it's amazing, a real work of art. I was going to ask him to come, but I thought he'd be overwhelmed with all this Lintott stuff going on today. I'll bring him next time – he's quite shy, very quiet. He's happiest just being at home, but I'll include him next time.'

'I hope he isn't offended that you didn't invite him this time, Henry! He made that special card, after all. Tell him we'd love to meet him. And what's his name? All I know is that you saved him from being crushed by someone's weight dropping on him in the gym, James told me.'

'Robert Burns, would you believe? His father's a Scotsman and a distant relative of the original Robert Burns, but my Robert goes by Robbie, which is what his mum always calls him. He's an accountant, who's also great at computer generated art.'

Then it was their turn to help themselves, and Mary spent the rest of the evening circulating among the family, catching up on news and doing a bit of surreptitious tidying in the kitchen to avoid everyone getting up to help. Leaving it all to the morning wasn't an option – their breakfast would be chaotic once again. But on her third trip to the kitchen end of the big room she found William's wife, Jo, helping Yolanta load the dishwasher. She put down the glasses she was holding and listened to their conversation and realised that Yolanta was making friends already.

And sometime in the future, she thought as she returned to the living room, we'll see if Robbie Burns can overcome his shyness and integrate into our crazy mob, provided he lasts until the next family event.

15

The minibus taxi arrived punctually, they all filed in and once everyone was seated Mary got in and stood beside the driver holding up a hand until everyone stopped talking. As usual she focused on Henry two rows down, to be able to speak without stammering, her old trick of coping with the mix of family and hangers-on.

'This is the last time we can fit into one minibus. The driver tells me he's making an exception, because we have more people than there are seats if we count the children. So every parent who's got a child on their lap must use the seat belt, but only on themselves, not around the child as well. Next time we'll have two minibuses or one bus and a taxi.'

She nodded at the driver and resumed her seat unaware that the rest of her family we're all looking at each other and laughing.

'The perfect planner! She future proofed it already,' said William to his wife who was sitting beside him with little Jane on her knee. 'I'm strapped in now, so pass Jane to me, so you can strap yourself in too. We'd better do what we've been told.' They shared a smile, and both looked at the back of Mary's head as she sat beside Archie in the front seat, completely unaware of the glances exchanged behind her.

Their arrival at Westmoreland's created the same stir as it always did. People stared as they walked in single file through the dining room, nudged each other and smiled. 'We're public property now,' said James and glanced back at Yolanta, who was behind him. 'You'll have to get used to this.'

'Totally acclimatised already - no need to worry about me.' Mary heard her and smiled. There was no need to worry about Yolanta not fitting in.

When they sat around the long table in the private dining room with Archie at the head, Mary got to her feet and once again fixed her eyes on Henry, her speech anchor. 'The menu has been decided in advance again, with a few options available. This time the choice of food is dad's because it's his birthday and I thought he should be able to have exactly what he likes best. There is a small section at the bottom of the menu with some special things for the children. Seeing none of the children have allergies they should be able to find something to suit their taste.'

She sat down and turned to James, who was on her right, and asked quietly if he had noticed the large flat parcel leaning against the wall at the far end of the room. 'Nobody brought it on the bus,' she said, 'so somebody had it delivered in advance. Do you know what it is?'

But James denied all knowledge and said there were probably only two people in the family who were capable of such trickery, when they had all agreed there shouldn't be any presents because Archie didn't want any. 'And that's you and Henry, so if it isn't you, it's got to be Henry.'

Marry laughed and thought that he was probably right. Right through the meal her eyes kept swivelling to the far corner where the parcel wrapped in plain brown paper leaned against the wall and in her head she tried to imagine what might be in it. A painting? A large photo of the family? As soon as their plates had been cleared after the main course William got to his feet and proposed a toast to Archie saying that he spoke for them all in expressing his hope that Archie would still be here 25 years from now, so they could all get together to celebrate his 100th birthday

'God knows how many there will be of us by then,' he said. 'We might need to book the whole restaurant for the evening, but I sincerely hope that the family will continue to get together for special occasions and teach our children what real family togetherness means.'

As soon as William sat down, Henry got up and went to fetch the large parcel. He rested it on his chair and stood behind it holding on to the top edge. 'I know we all agreed to abide by dad's wish not to buy him any presents, but I have disobeyed that instruction. Some of you know that I've got a new boyfriend, or partner if you like. He's a very clever chap, who besides being a management accountant is also an artist, a computer based artist, so to speak. His name is Robert Burns, and yes, I know that's quite funny, but it's true. He's a distant relation of the original Robert Burns, but he's usually called Robbie. He's heard me talk about this extraordinary family of ours and about what binds us together. How it started when Mary was a tiny baby without a mother and we all took turns feeding her and changing her and playing with her, and how that bond was indescribably strengthened after the abduction. I will never forget opening the boot of that abandoned car and lifting her out - a limp little body who hadn't had anything to eat or drink for twenty-six hours, and how Edward and I looked at each other and knew in that moment that we would never let anything happen to her again if we could possibly prevent it.'

He took a sip of his wine and continued with the glass in his hand. 'So Robbie, who thinks this is the most touching and uplifting story he has ever heard, started working on something without my knowledge – an artwork which he feels portrays what the Lintott tribe is about. This parcel contains three things, the first is the birthday card which we will all sign tonight. The image on the card is a small version of Robbie's artwork, which is why nobody has signed it yet, because I wanted dad to see it first. A big version of it is framed and that's the second thing in the parcel, and the third is a large print of the first Christmas photo dad took of us all lined up in front of the fireplace at home with Mopsy on William's arm, less than a year old and already with a head full of black curls.'

He put his glass down and started pulling the paper off the parcel. 'I'm doing this myself because I want to pass these things to dad one at a time.' He pushed his hand inside the wrappings, pulled out the card and walked around the table to hand it to his father. There was total silence while Archie studied the card for a long moment with a slightly confused look on his face, and Henry laughed. 'I know, dad! It's hard to see the detail on the card, but here is the big version in A3 format which shows all the minute details.'

He pulled it out of the parcel and walked to the end of the table and held it up so they could all see it. Against a grey background a mechanism that looked like the inside of an old fashioned clock was printed in dark gold. 'This is how Robbie sees our family though he's never met any of you yet. As you can see, this intricate mechanism surrounds a central little platform with a small girl sitting cross legged on it, a girl with curly black hair. And in various places linked by levers and cogwheels and chains are seven more platforms - all with a different sized male person on them, some sitting, some standing. I'm the one on the left, with my legs dangling over the edge of my platform. Dad is at twelve o'clock if I can describe it as that, as fits the head of the family, and us six brothers are spaced around, randomly, not according to age or size.'

He turned the artwork so they could all see it better and they studied it in total silence as Henry continued. 'To Robbie this represents how interlinked we are and how anything that happens to one of us effects the others. These levers and cogwheels mean that no one can do anything, nothing can happen to anyone in the family without the others being affected. I think this is a fabulous way of showing how this family works.'

He walked around the table again and handed the framed artwork to Archie who had tears running down his cheeks and was unable to get a word out.

'The staff here,' continued Henry, once again back at his chair with the glass in his hand, 'agreed in advance to take down two paintings that usually hang on that long wall over there, so we can hang these two for all of us to study closer when I've finally finished talking. I'll just hang the framed photo up right away. And last of all, and I nearly forgot. Robbie can print that artwork for anyone who would like a copy, either in that large size or smaller.'

The melee that followed after Henry hung the two works on the wall turned the room chaotic. Everyone got up to look, everyone commented and children asked to be lifted up, so they could see. Mary walked quietly out to confer with the head waiter. 'I'm s-sorry this has t-taken so long, but the presentation to my d-dad needed a lot of explaining. I hope none of the d-desserts have spoilt in the m-meantime, but if you think you can manage it, you could serve them n-now. Everyone is m-milling around, but I hope you can work around them.'

'No problem! Don't worry,' said Lucas, who knew Mary well. 'Henry warned us this would take some time, so seeing the speeches are over I'll get the staff to start serving dessert now.'

Once nearly everyone else was seated again Mary finally got a chance to study Robbie's picture and she was mesmerised. 'Incredible,' she said quietly to Henry, who had come to stand beside her. 'I would never have thought of it myself, but it's perfect – and so beautiful. Your Robbie is a genius, this is exactly how we are.' She turned her head to look at him and gave him a little jab with her elbow. 'And it precisely explains why my life is totally devoid of privacy.'

They both laughed and went back to their seats.

16

Ever since the lift incident Mary had at times felt confused and deeply unsettled. She had seen Gabriel four times, twice in the staff cafeteria, once in the lift and once in the corridor on her floor. These chance encounters were lodged in her mind like little video clips, and she played them back over and over, each time with the same feeling of disbelief. When their eyes met he gave her a little half smile or a nod and continued on his way without missing a beat. No slowing down and no hesitation, exactly as he would if they had only met briefly and never had a conversation, much less stood in a close hug in a dark room for fifteen minutes. This calm and nearly dismissive behaviour left her wondering if her instinctive feeling that Gabriel was strongly attracted to her and felt protective of her, was just her imagination.

Could it be that she felt so connected to him after the episode in the stationery room that she had imbued him with the same feeling without any foundation? But she dismissed this idea based on several things that in her mind confirmed that feeling of connection. She often picked up what she thought of as invisible hints in others, particularly men. Sometimes she was sure there was an underlying motive hidden behind a conversation, and nothing that man said or did could change the impression. And added to what she had sensed in Gabriel more than once, there was also her strong conviction that he was the one who had alerted her brothers about the harassment she was subjected to. Somehow he had known to contact John, and the line-up event was the result of his intervention, which resulted in John's suggestion that they all come on the Friday instead of piecemeal from Friday night to Saturday lunchtime, which had been an excuse, of course, so they could arrive early and do the Lintott line-up in the foyer at Tidwell's. Somehow Gabrial knew John from somewhere, but how was not the key question here, his decision to intervene was the main point and it fed into her feeling that he was attracted and felt he needed to protect her. This was the drawback of having a scientific mind and being trained to look objectively at the evidence, she told herself with a wry smile. It made it impossible for her to simply rely on her feelings and impressions without also taking into account other factors that might be contradictory to what she thought she had picked up from Gabriel.

These strange and conflicting thoughts and events continued to sit in the back of her mind. The little chain of events: being locked in that room, Gabriel mentioning that he knew about the bet those guys had on her, then the line-up. The way he had held her, his voice when he said, "let's turn you around" and clasped her to his chest, his hand running up through her hair. It was significant, she was sure of it. Something had developed between them nearly instantly, a close bond, as if they had known each other for a long time in some other time and place. It explained why she didn't stammer when she talked to him and why she had felt so safe being held by him. No feeling of strangeness when she stood all that time with her body tight against his and her face against the top of his chest. She could exactly recreate the temptation she had experienced, to lift her head just a little and put her mouth against the skin on his neck. But now his cool greetings frustrated her and stopped her even trying to talk to him when they met.

But taking that crucial step, from feeling nearly certain about him and actually doing something about it, was a big move that needed careful thought. When they stood outside the lift that day he had, without saying it, made it clear that he did not want their strange connection to develop further. But he had given her the little stone coin and said to hold it if she was alone in the dark and she had nearly heard his unspoken words "... when I'm not there to comfort you". Somehow she must resolve these conflicting impressions, because despite her science-trained mind she knew without a doubt they were meant to be much more than casual acquaintances. 'He *is* mine, I know he is,' she said to herself, as she waited for the bus one day and didn't realise she had spoken aloud until the woman beside her laughed and said, 'Of course he is!'

One evening when she was sitting on her bed watching a Korean drama on her laptop, unable to go to sleep, a disturbing thought popped into her head. Maybe Gabriel simply didn't like her, despite how protective and kind he had been in the stationery room. Perhaps there was something in her personality that put him off, perhaps it was her fear of the dark and being locked in. She tried to tell herself that thinking endlessly about Gabriel was a useless waste of time and mental energy, unless she could come up with a plan to do something about it, and she must stop dwelling on it.

On a glorious Saturday morning Mary stood irresolute outside the Sunflower Café in Barton Street after a text message from Ava saying she couldn't come after all, because her little sister had a netball game, and their mother was sick and couldn't take her. But here I am, she told herself, so why not go in? I can have a nice cup of coffee on my own and read on my phone, but I won't let myself be tempted to sit at an outside table now the sun is so hot. She opened the door, joined the line waiting to order and studied the cake cabinet beside her. Then without warning the man in front of her took a step backwards and bumped into her.

Without thinking Mary exclaimed, 'It's you!' and Gabriel swung around. She couldn't believe her luck, finally a chance to talk to him again. She was fully aware that this might be her best chance to have a proper conversation with him, because she couldn't confront him at work, where he never gave her a chance to pull him into a conversation, and here he couldn't evade her. Imagine, she thought and nearly smiled at the image in her mind, if I ran after him at work and grabbed hold of his arm and refused to let go! That would turn him right off and he'd probably take out a non-molestation order against me.

'Yes, it is,' was all he said in a way that was clearly intended to state that what she thought of as their close bond was not part of his world view. He looked perfectly calm and polite, with that kind of implied distance you adopt with people you hardly know and don't like. For a long moment she just stared into his face, trying to make up her mind what to say next. He saw her conflict and took pity on her. 'It was my fault. I stepped back suddenly when that waitress nearly dropped her tray trying to get past me.'

But now Mary couldn't think of what to say, how to start. Probably anything that came out of her mouth now would be wrong, and he would think she was mad and this opportunity would be ruined. Her feeling that he knew her so well, that he understood how closely linked they were, evaporated into thin air. It was all in her mind and she didn't know him at all. To him she was a little incident in the past, not important, and his kindness was just that, kindness, nothing more. Then the woman behind her made an impatient noise and she said quickly, 'Can I please talk to you?'

'You can join me,' was all he said, as if he was not particularly keen but would let her share his table as a favour.

'OK, then,' she said when they were seated opposite each other at a tiny round table, both with cups of coffee and, she noticed, both with a shortbread biscuit. She had thought about how to start their conversation while she ordered and decided that taking him by surprise and being abruptly up-front would be a good strategy to get him to engage and not just brush her off.

'Why don't you like me? Did I do something to offend you?' She held her breath now, nearly fearful, but hoping this direct approach might break through the barrier he had erected between them.

Surprise was clearly written on his face. 'Not *like* you? Why do you think I don't like you?'

'You never smile at me or talk to me at work. We see each other now and then, but you just kind of walk past as if we ... as if we don't really know each other. And I feel that we ... we know each other well, we understand each other.'

She didn't care how crazy this sounded, she had to get through to him. An opportunity like this might never come her way again. 'I know you talked to John – it had to be you. Those crazy brothers of mine wouldn't tell me who alerted them to do the line-up, but I know he organised it and he said he promised whoever it was not to tell me, but it must have been you. We talked about those guys who were after me, didn't we? When we were locked in. You kind of brought it up, and then you said we must exit separately to avoid gossip.'

There was no reaction from Gabriel, who was still hiding his thoughts behind a cool and slightly distant expression, so she continued. 'William wouldn't even tell me exactly what he and the CEO talked about. William's the oldest, twenty years older than I am. And he's a lawyer, so he knows how to sound serious.' Then she frowned. 'And if he knew how I'm hijacking your Saturday coffee he would seriously tell me off.'

He looked over her shoulder with an abstracted expression, and she waited for what he would say, half scared and half excited. 'The problem is that I like you too much,' he said finally and looked straight at her. 'Way too much! And I'm not for you, so I've tried to keep a distance. Call it self-protection.'

'But I like you too - way too much! Why do you say you're not for me? Are you married or something?'

'No, it's because I'm very hard to live with, so I try to never get seriously involved with anyone.'

'Why? Do you snore? Have you got a cleaning fixation and wipe every surface six times a day with antiseptic spray? Just exactly how hard are you to live with?' Suddenly she was enjoying herself. She knew what this was about now, and she wasn't going to give up. 'I'm pretty hard to live with, too. I stammer.'

'Not with me, you don't. You haven't stammered once since ...'

'Since you held me and comforted me and made me feel safe. I've missed that feeling so much! And then you were cold and distant in the office, even after you gave me your magical stone coin.'

She held out her hand and there it was, lying on the

palm of her hand, warm from her pocket. 'I carry it with me all the time, because you said it would help me, if something happens and I panic when you aren't around. Well, you didn't actually *say* that last bit, but it was written in a talk bubble above your head, so I know that's what you nearly said. I just got the stone out of my back pocket while I paid for my coffee, so I could show you.'

To her surprise he changed the subject. 'This thing about skin smells that you told me about after we met in the lift – it's unusual. I've never heard about it in humans before, though it happens with those dogs they train to scent certain illnesses.'

'You know what happened to me? Did John tell you? And don't try that innocent look with me! It won't work. You must have called him, though I can't understand how you knew how to find him.'

'I knew the moment you said you had six brothers. I saw the photo of the first Lintott line-up on social media when John and I were at university. He was a few years ahead of me, but we were both in the uni rugby team The hair is unmistakable, so thick and so black it's nearly blue – and curly. You had to be his sister, the little girl in the Facebook posts from years ago when they did the line-up at your school.'

They had both finished their coffee now, and she said without thinking of the consequences, 'Let's go for a walk in the park, and I'll tell you something nobody outside my family knows. I can't do it here, but I want you to know.'

To her surprised relief he nodded and led the way outside. In silence they walked the two blocks to the park and then slowly along one of the paths under the oaks where Mary deliberately steered them towards the little rise on the far side of the pond where few people went. 'How much do you know about what happened when I was abducted? Do you know how I was found?'

He glanced sideways and she could read his mind - he was worried that talking about this might upset her, and she felt his concern like a physical sensation, remembered how he'd held her in that dark room, and smiled. She knew without a doubt that she could tell this man anything, there were no barriers. And even if he didn't want her, she would always trust him and turn her thoughts to him if she was worried. 'There's no need to worry,' she said now. 'I don't ever talk about this in any detail, *never*, but I know I can with you.'

Oh, my God, she thought and felt a blush rising on her face, I constantly reveal too much to this man, but I can't help it and maybe it's the best strategy. All these things I'm saying might change his mind and make him realise that to me he's special and that he's not too hard to live with – not for me. He did say he liked me "way too much" and I could tell from his expression that he really meant it. I think he wants me as much as I want him.

Looking up at his face she could see he was pleased. Not that his expression had changed in any definitive way, but there was a little smile hovering somewhere in the background. They were in the direct sun now and instantly the back of her neck felt too hot. She reached back with both hands and lifted her hair to let the breeze cool her and noticed the way he looked at her when she did that. As if he wanted to take hold of her again and run his hand up through her hair. She pretended she hadn't noticed and he said, 'I know you were abducted and found, but that's all. It obviously affected you in a lasting way. Only tell me if you're sure it's not going to be too hard.'

So she told him, looking straight ahead and keeping her voice as steady as she could. This was the first time she had talked about this with anyone apart from her father and brothers.

'A man took me from our front garden when I was three and a half. I was out there like I was nearly every day unless it was raining, waiting for the postman, who was a friend of mine. Even when he didn't have mail for us he'd always stop by our gate and tell me something interesting, like how the black dog down the street was limping or he'd seen a cat high up in a tree, anything at all. And I would tell him something too, according to my dad, like how my porridge had been lumpy that morning or I had lost my best hairclip or something.'

She took a deep breath. 'But this other man appeared, and he just reached over and lifted me over the gate and threw me into the boot of his car, which turned out not to be his but stolen – and then he drove off. I remember clearly how my elbow hurt when he threw me down hard, and then he slammed the lid closed, and it was dark, completely black. And I lay there holding on to my sore elbow, but I can't remember what I thought, just how much my elbow hurt. He abandoned the car not far outside town, probably because a guy who was mowing his lawn two doors down from us saw him grabbing me and shouted and ran after the car. But he couldn't tell the police what kind of car it was, just that it was grey, he only saw it from behind.'

'How long was it until they found you? And who found you?'

She took another deep breath. 'Two of my brothers, Edward and Henry, found me twenty-six hours later. They had all been out searching. That man had driven the car off the road and into a clump of trees - everyone assumed he had gone much further, but my family decided to comb the entire area just in case.' She paused and thought for a moment. 'And maybe because they felt they needed to do something, anything at all.'

She took another deep breath. 'While I was locked into that dark space, alone and scared and not understanding why it had happened, I think I felt I would be there forever, with no light and no food and no water. I didn't think of death, because I didn't know anything about dying, I was too young. And after I was found I didn't trust anybody. *Nobody*, apart from my family. I thought that everyone was dangerous, there was no such thing as being safe, apart from with my dad and my brothers.'

She paused again and he seemed to know she was not finished and said nothing. 'I didn't understand in such detail what it was I felt all those long hours while I was locked in that dark space, but in retrospect I've identified the feeling – it was total despair, that it would never end, that I would be alone in the dark forever. That's what I re-lived in the stationery room, and you fixed it. You now represent complete safety and total trust, just like my brothers do. It doesn't matter what *you* say or feel about it - that's just how it is and how it will always be. You belong to me.'

She finally looked at him, and she could read the body language. He had to struggle to not take hold of her, he kept his hands by his sides by sheer willpower to stop himself reaching for her. She knew it without a doubt and held her breath in anticipation. But he reined in his reaction and said quite calmly, 'Your mother must have been going out of her mind.'

'There is – and was - no mother in our family.' She realised how crazy that sounded. 'The woman, who was my brothers' mother, died of cancer and my dad remarried. So I'm a half-sister. And then *my* mother left when I was just ten months old and never came near us again. She went back to Canada where she was from.' She nearly smiled. 'Dad always says she was too young to cope with all those big boys.' After a brief pause, she added, 'He did tell her I was missing, but she didn't come.'

Should she mention it? Or would it create that block on her ability to speak that sometimes happened when someone tried to find out the more intimate details of the abduction. And she realised that even the fact that she could think calmly about it meant that of course she could mention it, she could tell this man anything.

'Sometimes people try to pry into the details,' she said looking straight ahead again, intent on sounding calm. 'They want to know what that man did to me – it's what my brother Rick calls "prurient interest". It's a perverted wish to revel in something deviant and sexual with no thought for how it affects me. But the answer is no, he did nothing to me apart from lock me in that dark space for twenty-six hours. After that lid slammed closed I never saw him again, and I have no impression of what he looked like – it was all too quick. He did nothing sexual to me, but he had probably planned to. My stammer and fear of the dark is just a remnant of being locked up for so long, alone in the dark, helpless and hopeless, but nothing physical.'

She could feel his eyes on her, but she didn't turn her head. 'I have never said that to anyone before apart from to my family. Not to doctors or police trauma people or anyone. And don't ask me why, I have no idea why it's such a touchy thing. Probably it's the invasion of privacy or maybe it's that even from that young age I sensed something secondary when they asked me, so I refused to answer. I just let dad and the boys tell the authorities that he hadn't touched me after he threw me into the boot.'

He stopped and turned to look directly at her face, a searching gaze that felt intense, though his expression was calm, and she smiled again. 'Don't panic! I have been surrounded by love

and attention from all those guys all my life, since I was a baby
– they brought me up from the day my mother left, and I've
never missed having a mother, I've always been protected.
They treated me as a pet or a doll – and they're still like that.'

She more sensed than saw the movement of his hand, as
if he had once again nearly reached out to touch her, but
again he restrained himself, so she continued as if she hadn't
noticed. 'But anyway, when Ed and Henry found me, I
refused to let go of Henry, who lifted me out of that car, he
was nineteen or twenty at the time. Nobody could prise me
out of his arms for several hours. I just clung on, wet panties
and all, and he held me. For the next several days I was
passed from one set of arms to the next, day and night, and
I don't think my feet touched the floor once, apart from
when they carried me to the toilet. The fed me and washed
me while I sat on someone's knee, changed my clothes, told
me stories, and I slept on someone's lap, and so it went.
After a couple of days I let Henry take me into the shower,
sill carrying me, and we stood there under the warm water
for ages – I can still remember how lovely it felt.' She
paused and thought of Henry singing to her while the water
cascaded over them and that she had giggled at how he still
in his shorts on and he had hugged her closer.

'They had all come home the moment they heard I was
missing.' She looked up at Gabriel again. 'And it was lucky
they did instead of relying on the official search, which had
branched out much further from the city.'

They were still standing facing each other and now she

took a couple of steps closer, right up so her face was mere inches away from the top of his chest.

'And I somehow learnt the smell of their skin, being held like that day and night, like I developed a sixth sense. I didn't need to open my eyes, I knew who was holding me – and I still do. It's nothing to do with being clean or not, or any products they've used – it's the underlying scent their bodies produce. And now I could find *you* in a crowd of males in the dark, too.' She moved even closer and put her hand on his chest. 'Would you please hold me, just for a moment?'

She had taken him totally by surprise, she could feel how taken aback he was, and though she had not deliberately ambushed him, she was pleased she had taken that extra step closer and asked. After only a second's hesitation his arms closed around her and once again he pulled her close, and she leaned against his chest and buried her face in his shoulder. One of his hands slid up the back of her neck under her hair, and then further until his fingers cupped her head and held her against him. A flare of desire swept down her body, and she could feel it coursing through him too. For a brief moment his head rested against hers, then abruptly he released her and took a step back, and she nearly fell over.

'No!' he said and sounded nearly angry. 'This is not going to happen! We'll both end up hurt, so let's say we're friends, but we're not having any more hugs.'

She was lost for words. The sudden change from that intense flash of mutual desire, and the feel of his hand sliding through her hair, to this – it left her with no idea what to say, but he continued before she managed to get a word out. 'Don't say anything, please, and don't tempt me again. I told you I'd be too hard to live with, and I mean it, so let's not start anything.'

He turned and walked off and left her standing there staring after him. 'You just wait, you idiot man! This isn't something you can walk away from,' she said out loud to his retreating back, though he was probably already too far away to hear her. 'Do you think I didn't feel how you reacted when we hugged? I'm not stupid. I *know* you belong to me, and you've got no idea how stubborn I am.'

She stood there with plans and ideas tumbling through her mind, determined to find a way to overcome his ultimatum. He knew she wanted him, and she was certain that he wanted her, too, it had been perfectly clear when he held her. That short hug just now had told her a lot and made her more certain than ever. But she needed a strategy, some way of making him realise that he wouldn't be too hard to live with, not for her, at any rate.

It didn't take a lot of imagination to work out what had led to this unshakeable belief that he would be too hard to live with. It couldn't just be that he felt his scar was too off-putting, there had to be more too it. It must be that at some stage a woman had either rebuffed him in a brutal way based on his scarred face, or someone he lived with had left, possibly shared horrible comments about him on social media. She subsided on a park bench and sat for a long time staring straight ahead without noticing anything, totally intent on working out how to show him he was wrong.

17

A couple of days after going for that revealing and frustrating walk with Gabriel, Mary decided to call Mrs Wong to try to sort something out. For days she had struggled with a depressing feeling that this project was bound to go wrong. But standing at her bedroom window that morning she had finally worked out what her strategy would be. Somehow sitting on her bed or in the living room and trying to think of some constructive way to help Mrs Wong had produced nothing that seemed remotely workable. Every idea she came up with was doomed to failure for one reason or another, Mrs Wong's reputed personality not the least important consideration. But standing there by the open window looking out over the big garden, watching the tuis feasting on kowhai flowers along the back fence, had reset her thinking and given her an idea that might work. The worst thing that could happen would be that Mrs Wong said no, she'd changed her mind and didn't want any help, or that she lost her temper or felt insulted. But the sudden inspiration about what to suggest that struck her that morning would give them both the opportunity to go forward in stages, change the plan and work something out if the original idea didn't work.

Mary was sitting alone at a little table in the staff cafeteria, a large room with a huge Italian coffee machine, a vending machine full of nutbars and chips, with groups of tables and chairs scattered and frequently rearranged when bigger groups moved chairs or pushed tables together. The dynamics of how this room changed had fascinated her from the start, but today she was nearly the only person there. She had taken a late break after deciding to finish a big data entry job that Debbie wanted done as soon as possible, and today this room that was usually crowded was quiet and calm, empty apart from two men in the far corner, both busy with their phones.

So she called Mrs Wong and was surprised at how positive she sounded, nearly excited. 'Oh, yes! Maylene said she'd ask you to call. It will be lovely to see you again, I haven't seen you for years, not since you were a teenager. Why don't you come and have a glass of wine after work. Do you know the address?'

Wow, very surprising, thought Mary, far more positive than I had expected. I was nearly sure she would have changed her mind by now. Maybe she doesn't remember *why* I'm calling? 'Could you send me a t-text message – I haven't got a p-pen handy right now. You can see my phone number in your c-caller list. Is that OK?'

In the back of her mind she thought it was quite likely that Mrs Wong didn't send messages and maybe didn't know how to save someone's contact details, so she added quickly, 'Or I can send you a message now, so you just need to reply.'

'Oh no, I'll save your details, so I have them, and then I'll message you the address. Maylene told me where you work. You need to take the number 61 bus eastwards from the centre of the city, so you don't have to change at Bridge Street. And don't take the 64 or you'll have to change twice.'

And true to her word, a few minutes later Mrs Wong's message arrived on Mary's phone, and she sat for a moment trying to decide how to broach the subject of the messy house, if Mrs Wong had forgotten the reason for the visit, a prospect that seemed likely after this warm welcome.

'Mary! It's so lovely to see you!' said Mrs Wong when she opened her front door to Mary's knock. She was short and a lot chubbier than last time Mary saw her and her smile signalled real pleasure. 'Come in! You know it's messy, Maylene said she'd told you.'

She led the way down the hall to the kitchen where two wine glasses and some snacks were set out on the little table beside the window. 'Would you like red wine or white?'

'R-red, please.'

With the wine poured Mrs Wong handed Mary a glass and said, now sounding slightly hesitant, 'Do you want to see the mess now or after we've had our wine?'

'Let's have a quick l-look now and then we c-can have the wine and discuss what t-to do. If that's OK with you?'

When Mrs Wong flung the living room door open and stood aside, Mary stopped in the doorway and nearly took a step back. Never in her life had she seen anything like it - calling it a mess was a serious understatement. It really was hoarding, just as Maylene had said. There was nowhere to sit because every surface was covered with – what? She looked around and tried to take it in, analyse what was there. Boxes, courier bags, things stacked on top of each other, and all of it interspersed with clothing, bits of which poked out from under things. The floor was not much better, and the total area free to walk on was probably only a couple of square metres, if that.

'You see? It's a disaster and I don't know where to start,' said Mrs Wong and now her voice was trembling. 'I know it's my own fault, but it's too much for me now. I can't think of how to sort it out, or how to even start.' She cleared her throat. 'I feel overwhelmed just thinking about it, so I just don't get started. I just close this door and ...'

Mary took one tentative step into the room and turned to smile reassuringly at Mrs Wong, who had tears in her eyes. 'I have an idea that m-might sound a bit s-silly, but I think it m-might work. Let's go b-back to our wine and have a chat about it once I've had a quick l-look around.'

A minute or two was enough to tell her that there had been no system in how things were deposited, they had simply been put down randomly, in the first space that caught the eye. A porcelain ornament, a crinoline clad lady leaning on a staff with a lamb at her feet, lay precariously on top of a sliding pile of bubble wrap, which in turn seemed to be resting on a stack of dinner plates. That's an armchair under there, thought Mary, I can just see the bottom of it, and that mound over there is a side table nearly completely hidden under some clothes and what looks like a box full of books. There was nothing to be gained by further study, so she turned back to Mrs Wong and smiled. 'Wine t-time, I think!'

They retreated to the kitchen and Mrs Wong took a big swallow of her wine, set the glass down with a bang and fixed her gaze on Mary. 'Do you think we can work out how to do it?'

'Oh yes, of course we c-can. I think m-my plan will do it – not in one g-go but over a couple of weeks perhaps? Maylene said we have p-plenty of time. So, this is what I thought.' She had made a mental adjustment to her plan when she saw the amount of plastic, polystyrene and other packaging, and now the first step of the plan would become the second – the packaging had to be managed first.

Trying to make it seem like a social visit, she reached for the bowl of peanuts and took a few. 'Now, you stop m-me if you think my p-plan is crazy, OK? This is what we could do – first I c-come over on Saturday morning and we spend a couple of hours sorting out the p-packaging. We roll up the b-bubble wrap, fold the p-paper and flatten the boxes - just generally clear m-most of it out. Do you have room in your g-garage to store it? Just so we d-don't get rid of stuff that would b-be useful to wrap things in later.'

'Oh, yes, the garage isn't in a mess. I never put anything in there apart from the car.'

She drank some more wine and looked expectantly at Mary, who quietly wondered why everyone said Mrs Wong was so difficult. Or perhaps it would manifest itself at a later date and force her to come up with a different plan or even retreat from the project.

'G-good! And then step t-two is a day-by-day thing. Every day you fill a small b-box I'll get from the s-supermarket, and I'll give you a new one when I p-pick up the one you've filled that d-day. Put anything in that you don't really need, it doesn't m-matter what it is. I take the full b-box away and you fill another the next d-day. Just one box each day. If it's something that won't f-fit in the box you text me and I'll b-bring a bigger one or just p-put stuff in my car. Do you think that would work f-for you?'

The pause lasted a long time. Mrs Wong sat there with a pensive look on her face and her gaze out the window, but finally her eyes swung back to Mary, and she asked unexpectedly, 'Why do you keep calling me Mrs Wong?'

It made Mary laugh. 'Because that's what I always used t-to do. I don't think I've ever heard your f-first name - and when we last m-met I was much younger and didn't call anyone's p-parents by their Christian name.'

'Please call me Pat! I have a Chinese first name, of course, and so do my children, but I never use it. I've been called Pat or Patsy by everyone since I started school. What were you thinking of doing with the things in those boxes I give you?'

Mary had thought of this, and she hoped her solution would find favour. 'I thought that anything which m-might be useful for the Women's Refuges could g-go to them, you know, things those women m-might find useful, the ones who've had to abandon everything to get away from their p-partners. And other things could go into a g-garage sale, either here or at my place. What do you think?'

'That's a good idea - and it's nice to think that ome of it would be useful to other people. I hadn't thought of the Refuge, but they probably need more supplies all the time. And the Salvation Army too, they have a place over in Valley Road where they have household things they give to people who can't afford to buy new stuff.'

'And a garage sale would earn you some m-money, too.' Mary grinned. 'But you'd have to p-promise me not to spend it in a second-hand shop again or online. Maylene said your n-new flat is much smaller.'

'I won't, I promise! I haven't bought anything for ages. It was just for a year or so after ...' She paused. 'I got depressed when my husband left me and I was very sad after Liam moved out, but he hated the mess.' She paused again and looked down. 'He said it made him feel ill, and he had to go and live somewhere else. And I couldn't ask him to help me sort things out, he couldn't handle it.'

Mary left half an hour later with a huge sense of relief. Taking on something so personal and so potentially tricky with someone she didn't know well had worried her, and she had only agreed because she knew how difficult the Wong family thought it would be to get things sorted out. Perhaps they didn't realise how depressed Pat was, or perhaps had been, she thought as she waited for the bus to her own suburb, and Pat might have felt they were critical and that made her stroppy, like anyone might in that situation. She got her phone out sent a long text message to Maylene instead of calling her, which would have taken too much time - ending a phone conversation with her sometimes took a long time, and she wanted to think through what she might need on Saturday. She ended the message saying, "We've agreed on a plan, we start on Saturday morning, but please don't join us! We need to make a start, just the two of us first and get into a routine. I'll keep you informed."

On Saturday morning Mary left home at eight and spent half an hour in the supermarket picking up boxes of different sizes, put them in the car and continued to the café just down the road from Pat's house, which she had noticed the first time she came. After a moment's thought outside Pat's house she decided to only bring the morning tea and lunch inside and leave the boxes in the car, so as not to overwhelm her.

'I b-brought some lunch and something n-nice to have with coffee.' She handed her the bags. 'I thought we c-could do a little bit of sorting before we have m-morning tea perhaps?'

'Oh, you shouldn't have!' Pat opened one of the bags on the way to the kitchen. 'Oh, nice! Those little pastries are my favourites. I'll put the jug on right away.'

Mary left her in the kitchen and went to study the living room again. We'll start at this end closest to the door, she decided, and just move as much of the packaging as we can into the hall or outside and take it straight out to my car. All the bits and pieces we find underneath we'll have to put somewhere to sort out later, maybe on the windowsills and on whatever surface appears when we move things. I hope I've got enough string to tie around the bubble wrap until I find some recycling place that will take it, it's far more than I remembered.

She returned to the kitchen and realised it looked different, but before she could comment Pat said, 'I can see you've noticed. I made a start in here, moved everything back into cupboards and drawers and cleared the benches. Good, eh?' Then she made a face and shook her head. 'I thought I might do something in the living room or the bedroom too, but I just couldn't decide where to start. I just closed the door and decided to wait until you were here.'

'Is there m-more stuff to sort in the b-bedrooms?'

Pat nodded. 'Just in the guest room, the one that used to be Maylene's room. Liam's room is just as he left it.' She turned away to make the coffee. She hoped he might come back, thought Mary, so she left his room as it was. The poor woman! And since Liam left she's lived here alone and just given up. She mentally readjusted the timeline for the project and heaved a silent sigh.

18

The text message arrived just as Mary was getting off the bus, but she ignored the ping from her phone because the woman in front of her tripped on the uneven pavement and fell forward quite hard, her head hitting the ground. Marry jumped off the steps and knelt beside her.

'L-let me help you up.' The woman raised herself to a kneeling position with both hands on the ground and turned her head, and Mary realised that she was quite badly hurt. Blood was running down her face from above her eye, and it looked as if she had split her eyebrow open.

'I think you'd b-better have that seen to,' said Mary and put a hand the woman's elbow to help her up from the ground. 'That's a very n-nasty wound, I think it probably n-needs stitches.'

'Here, take this,' said a voice behind her and a hand pushed a wad of tissues into her hand. Pressing the tissues hard against the woman's eyebrow Mary turned to the man behind her. 'Do you think we should call f-for an ambulance?'

'I'll take her,' he said. 'I live only a couple of steps from here. I'll get my car now and drive her to the hospital, that wound definitely needs stitches. I am a nurse at the hospital, and I can get her seen immediately in the emergency department.'

'Yes please,' were the first words the woman had said since she fell. 'That's very kind of you - I don't want all the fuss with an ambulance.'

The man jogged off, the bus left and Mary waited until the man returned with his car.

This little drama had driven the text alert out of her mind, and she didn't notice it until half an hour after she got home, when she had washed her hands and got her phone out of her pocket. The message was from Ava: "Call me when you have time. We missed our date the other day but I have something hilarious to tell you.'

Mary sat down at the kitchen table and made the call straight away. She couldn't wait to hear what Ava had to tell her. She sometimes related little incidents from her work and Mary had never known if she also told others, or if she was the chosen recipient for Ava's confidences.

'Hi,' she said and pressed the speaker button. 'What's up?'

'Promise you'll never tell anyone! This is the cutest and funniest thing that's happened to me for ages. You know how I had to take my baby sister to netball practice? And of course I watched the session, so I could drive her home afterwards. Guess what she said!'

This exclamation was quite unusual for Ava who was rarely so cheerfully chatty. 'I c-can't even imagine. What d-did she say?'

'She asked me to find someone she could practise kissing on! Isn't that the cutest thing you've ever heard?'

Marry smiled, amused and surprised at the same time. 'How old is she?'

'Just turned fourteen a week ago- and when I asked her why she needed to practise kissing, she said that soon she'll be going on dates and she wants to be prepared, so she's good at it.'

They both laughed, but Mary wondered if Ava really had suggested someone for her sister to practise kissing with – it seemed a bit strange. 'You're n-not going to hand her over to some k-kissable police colleague, are you?'

'God, no! Don't be silly, that would be child trafficking. I just told her to ask some boy she knows, someone she's good friends with and trusts, to give her lessons, but she said she doesn't know any boys who have kissable mouths.'

'This is the funniest thing ever,' said Mary when they had stopped laughing. 'So what d-did you suggest?'

'I told her to wait until she falls in love with someone, and when she does, whatever his mouth looks like won't matter. She will still want to be kissed by him.'

'Or by *her*,' said Mary. 'She might be like you and fall in love with a girl.'

There was a long pause from Ava. 'You know, I never thought of that! How funny!'

'You know how you s-sometimes tell me things in c-confidence – am I your safe storage b-box where you keep secrets?'

'You always have been,' said Ava comfortably. 'Ever since I first met you through Andrea when you were twelve or so. You're the only person I know I can trust with stuff like this. Remember when I told you about my experiment with that guy I met in the nightclub a couple of years ago? When I thought I'd see if I was possibly bi-sexual and not just queer, because I kind of felt drawn to him in a way I hadn't experienced with a man before? That disastrous date we went on - God, that was the worst! I hadn't thought of it in ages. You're literally the only person in the world who knows that story.'

'I'm very f-flattered, thank you! And p-please let me know if there are any further developments on the k-kissing front! Such a sweet story.'

When Archie came in from golf she was cutting up chicken to make a Thai dish with cashew nuts with her ear pods in and didn't hear him until he turned up right beside her.

'Andew died this morning,' he said and she could see his sadness. 'That's another one gone – I suppose when you're my age your friends become fewer with every year.'

Mary didn't know quite how to respond to this, so instead of commenting she asked, 'How old were your parents when they died?'

He thought for a moment, and she watched his face and thought what a handsome man he was with his thick grey curly hair and deep brown eyes until he said, 'My mother was ninety-two and my father was ninety-one, I think, or maybe he was ninety-two as well. And uncle Jack lived to at least ninety, but I can't remember exactly. He was miles older than my dad and it's a long time since he passed.'

'Well, you've got a great genetic profile then,' said Mary casually and turned on the heat under the wok. 'Can you pass me the canola oil please? You'll probably live to a hundred or more like William said on your birthday.'

After dinner, when her father went outside to take the rubbish trundler to the gate for next morning's collection, Mary dug out a box of chocolates they had been given some time ago, put six on a saucer on the table for Archie and took a few with her to her bedroom. She heard him come in and call out a 'thanks!' before she put her headphones on and turned on the final episode of the Korean drama she was watching on her laptop.

That night she had a dream that was so realistic that when she woke up with a start, she wasn't sure what was reality and what she had imagined. She got out of bed and met her father in the hallway.

'Did you hear that terrible bang? I wasn't sure if it was real or in my dream,' she said. 'It might have been something falling off the scaffolding next door. It's been making creaky noises when the wind comes up. Oh no, listen!'

They both headed for the front door and the sight that met their eyes when they opened it was far more alarming than a piece of scaffold falling from next door's roof. The night was full of loud voices; a car lay upside down on the sidewalk and people in PJs and dressing gowns were coming out of houses up and down the street.

The ensuing chaos of people helping the two in the car to get out through the missing windscreen, calling instructions to each other, and then the sudden shouted warning when someone smelt petrol. It was a drama impossible not to watch and it kept Archie and Mary standing shivering on their front doorstep.

'No point in us trying to help,' said Mary. 'There are far too many people out there already and I've already done my good Samaritan duty today.'

They remained on the step watching as ambulances and a fire truck arrived and while they stood there Mary told her father about the little drama at the bus stop, then gradually things quieted down. But going back to sleep proved to be difficult. Not only had adrenalin coursed through her body when she jerked awake an hour earlier, but the dream was hard to dismiss. I wish I could dream it again, she whispered to herself, as she lay there wide awake looking at the shadows from the neighbour's apple tree outlined on her blind. She wished she could dream it again every single night, it had made her feel so happy. To relive that quarter of an hour in the stationery room with Gabriel, to feel his strong arms around her and his hand holding her head against his shoulder, to hear his heartbeats, the feeling of absolute trust. The warmth that emanated from his body was a physical memory she could nearly recreate by thinking about it. She tried to bring back what it felt like when he supported her full weight against him, but what had seemed so real in the dream eluded her and she failed to capture it.

19

One morning in late October, when a surprisingly early summer seemed to have settled in for good, Mary looked out of her bedroom window and decided to wear her new top. Ava had persuaded her to buy a bright turquoise T-shirt when they went to the mall together the previous weekend.

'Now that you've been brave enough to wear that lime green shirt Andrea talked you into, I think you should continue being adventurous. You look stunning in bright colours – you need to stop trying to blend into the background.'

At the time Mary had wondered if Andrea and Ava had discussed this and made a plan to change her habits a little. Thinking back she recalled a few comments over the last year or so about how quietly she dressed. Not criticism, more like casual little half-joking comments made in passing. Now she studied her image in the mirror and decided it worked, even if it felt slightly over the top – such a bright colour with her black hair and brown eyes. But why not? It was just that she had never worn bright colours and maybe it was time to break the habit.

'Great colour – you look gorgeous!' said Debbie when Mary arrived. 'I'm so pale I never wear really bright things – they kind of overwhelm me and my face simply disappears.' She looked down at her pale pink shirt and laughed. 'Could you please help Graham this morning – I've asked him to apply some logic in that damn stationery room. Gretchen and I decided it's got to get done, it should have been sorted out a couple of years ago, at least. I checked with IT and they said they'll put anything that's not still useful on the floor tomorrow morning, so it can go to the special recycling place at Corbley.'

After a morning spent putting piles of things on the floor in the corridor, moving other things and making decisions about what should go into the big recycling wheelie bin that Graham had brought inside. They went to have a late lunch, leaving several piles along the wall of the corridor for Graham to take out to the rubbish dumpster in the back yard after lunch.

'Don't panic but Stuart wants to talk to you,' said Debbie when they returned to the admin office. 'You know where his office is?'

'Stuart?'

'Sorry, Stuart Ford, the CEO. Go up to the fifth floor, turn right when you get out of the lift and you'll see his door open at the end of the corridor. He's waiting for you, he called five minutes ago.'

What could this possibly be about? wondered Mary and headed for the lift. Surely the top guy wouldn't bother about something a junior admin person had done wrong. She hadn't set eyes on him since the day of the line-up when he came down to the foyer to talk to William. Maybe it was something to do with that awful bet, maybe one of those horrible guys had made up some kind of complaint about her. She paused at the top of the stairs, squared her shoulders and marched down the passage toward the open door at the end, mentally preparing herself to be calm and decisive. I'd resign rather than get involved in any type of workplace trouble, she thought, but I mustn't do anything impulsive, or I might never get a chance to talk to Gabriel again.

'Come in and sit down, Mary,' said the CEO, and if his smile was anything to go by, this was not about trouble. 'I've asked Bertrand to join us, but he'll be a few minutes. I've just discovered that you have a science degree, and you majored in biochemistry, is that right?'

'Yes, I g-graduated l-last year.'

'So, why did you apply for a clerical job?'

She could tell he was genuinely interested, but the question was slightly confusing, surely it was obvious. 'There wasn't anything available in the l-lab or relating to the chemistry d-department, so I applied f-for the junior clerical job to be able to at least work here.' She smiled. 'I thought maybe some useful information would come m-my way even in that job – help me d-decide if I should go b-back and do a master's degree, and what subject I might choose f-for my thesis, if I do.' She thought for a moment and added. 'I've always b-been interested in what your c-company does, so I thought just being in the b-building would be a chance.'

He nodded at someone in the doorway behind her and a tall, gangly man with a shock of grey hair appeared beside Mary and sat down in the other chair.

'This is Bert, who leads the research teams, he's ultimately in charge of the laboratories. I told him about you on the phone a few minutes ago, and he said he'd be keen to talk to you straight away.'

Bertrand turned to her with a grin on his deeply lined face. 'Couldn't resist the offer of a junior slave, could I? The Section 2 lab is screaming for help, so this is like a gift from the gods. They're flat out after Jayden left and Donna started her chemo, and she won't be back for months, so Wendy will be delighted.' He noticed the look on Mary's face. 'Donna is a lab technician, and Wendy is my second-in-charge. I know you've probably had holiday jobs in the industry while you've been a student, so there'll be a lot of stuff you're competent to do, and we'll train you further, too. Lots of scope for a curious mind.'

'Thank you!' She gave him a wide smile. 'This is so exciting! But I d-don't think Debbie will be p-pleased – we're so b-busy at the moment, I've been running around like c-crazy all week.'

'Never mind what Debbie thinks,' said the CEO. 'She can hire another clerk, they're easy to get. I'm glad I found out about your degree, though. I knew Bert was going to need another pair of hands, and I knew you had done chemistry, so I asked for your CV. I must admit I felt it was meant to be when I saw you've completed your degree.'

Could she ask? Yes, she decided, she must because this was so strange. 'How d-did you know I was studying chemistry?'

'William told me when those amazing brothers of yours came for their famous visit.' He glanced at Bertrand and they both started laughing. 'We're not laughing at you – it's just those videos. We all keep watching the Lintott line-up videos online, particularly the one someone started filming before they even got in the door. Must have been someone here, who was forewarned and ready. That footage is being shared everywhere, and my daughter is mesmerised by it – she says it's the most amazing thing she's ever seen. They're an impressive lot, your brothers.'

Bertrand turned to Mary and sounded genuinely apologetic. 'And I have to confess that I was the one, who then found the old video of the line-up at your high school, when your brothers went to scare the bullies, and now that's being shared everywhere again. It's very striking, that schoolyard full of kids standing like frozen and totally silent.'

Seeing how surprisingly casual they were Mary decided they might like to know the background. 'The line-up is a thing m-my dad got them into. He t-takes a photo every Christmas of them lined up like that with m-me in the middle. In the v-very first one William was twenty and I was l-less than a year old.'

'Great tradition,' said Stuart. 'Now, back to business and whatever Debbie feels doesn't matter, as I just said.

She knows the labs have priority, so tomorrow you report to Bert, start time eight o'clock. I'll get Gretchen to organise a key card for the lab floor for you to pick up in the morning when you arrive, and I'll tell the HR manager to give you a new contract. I think that's all that needs to be done.'

When Mary and Bertrand got up to leave, Stuart got up too and came around his desk. 'I was appalled when William told me about the harassment and the plans those guys had. The one who works here has been given a formal warning and he swears it won't happen again with anybody. I think I've made him understand how that kind of thing would affect a woman and how unacceptable it is.' He frowned. 'And I've informed the other company that we've had trouble with three of their employees - told them the details and asked that they be dealt with too.'

Mary returned to the admin department with her mind in a whirl. Now she would have an interesting job, learn lots of new things and her pay would be higher. She couldn't wait to tell the boys. They'd be so pleased for her, and so would Archie.

That Debbie already knew was clear from the way she shook her head when Mary walked in. 'This is sad – I'm very sorry to lose you! You're such a good worker, but needs must when the devil drives, as they say. Oh, delete that please! I didn't mean Stuart! Bert said you'll start on the lab floor tomorrow. I bet you're pleased.'

'God, yes, it's such a v-valuable opportunity. But I'd b-better get g-going with that next lot of d-data entry right away, so I get it done today.'

The next day was an initiation into a different world, far removed from her previous world involving photo copiers, stationery cupboards and mostly very simple routine tasks. Gretchen in reception gave Mary an ID card on a lanyard when she arrived and showed her how to put the key card on the scanner to open the door to get into the lab section.

'Make sure you put it right against the scanner,' she said. 'Don't just hold it in front, it won't work if it doesn't touch. Ask for Wendy, she'll show you around. She's Bert's second in command and heads up Section 2.'

Entering the laboratory floor was like coming into a different world. As Wendy led her through the long corridor Mary glanced into glass-walled rooms where personnel in white coats or protective overalls worked at benches or machinery. One door had a sign indicating that everybody who entered must wear a respirator mask.

With a white coat on and the lanyard around her neck, Wendy pronounced Mary ready for the tour of the laboratories and offices, which turned out to be very thorough and took a surprisingly long time. The first stop was in the staff changing room where everyone on the lab floor had a locker. On the wall was a line of signs with the symbols used in laboratories all over the world.

'They're on doors all through this floor and they're important. This symbol means there's positive air pressure inside the room to prevent stray organisms getting in.' Wendy grinned. 'Which, of course, you know with your degree behind you, but I'm obliged to point out absolutely everything that relates to health and safety. And that one is for spaces where you have to wear a regular mask, then the one about respirators, then that last one about gloves and hazard overalls.'

She turned and faced Mary to make sure she took this seriously. 'I know you've worked in labs before, but we have an extra system here which we stick to religiously. Anyone who wants to talk to someone in a high-hazard lab has to use the communication module on the wall by the door. Never open the door, just wait for someone to come to the door and talk to you.'

After going through the row of signs one by one they continued to where protective equipment was kept, where the toxic waste bins were and what not to do inside rooms with gas cylinders. 'Particularly hydrogen and oxygen,' Wendy pointed out. 'Not that anyone's allowed to smoke anywhere in the building, but we have to be super careful, so please don't bring a me cake with lit candles for my birthday or someone will turn the fire extinguisher on you.'

They continued along another corridor, where they met Bert frowning and talking on his phone, and arrived at a corner room with comfortable chairs around small tables and another giant silver coffee machine, just like the one in the staff cafeteria two floors down. They do look after their staff, thought Mary, and looked around to see if there was a vending machine here too but apparently not.

'Time for a break! Now's the time to ask me questions, and then I'll tell you where you'll be starting after lunch and what you'll be doing. IT is sending a guy down at twelve to set you up with the necessary logon details for the systems we run here. They're different from the ones used in rest of the building, of course, because we have specialised software of various kinds. You're probably already familiar with some of them from holiday placements.'

That will be that Scots guy who'll come, thank God he didn't see me in the stationery room, thought Mary. Imagine the stories he might have told all over the place if he'd seen me!

But it was Gabriel, who came down from IT, and his look of surprise when he realised who needed logons proved that he hadn't had any idea she had been moved to the laboratories.

'Let me introduce you two, and then I'll leave you to it,' said Wendy. 'Mary, this is Gabriel, head of IT, who rarely, if ever, honours us with a visit.' She grinned. 'But here he is! And this is Mary Lintott, who's just been moved to us from admin after Stuart found out she has a degree in biochemistry – a blessing for us, but Debbie in admin wasn't pleased to lose her. She needs access to all the usual stuff, LIMS, ChemDraw and Gaussian. Sorry I've got to leave you to it. Mary's going to be at Donna's desk in the open office, I'll be in lab 3 if you need me.'

And there they stood, both momentarily struck dumb, but Gabriel recovered first. 'Why were you in admin if you have a chemistry degree?'

She had to restrain herself from taking a step closer, and she knew he had noticed the impulse. 'There wasn't an opening in the labs when I first tried to get a job here, so I thought any job here would be worth it – which turned out to be right.'

'OK,' said Gabriel when he had logged on to the

computer on her desk and opened a screen she had never seen when she worked in the administration office. He got up and gestured for her to sit. 'You see the software icons on the screen, up there to the left. Click on ChemDraw first and I'll tell you the next step.'

Throughout the process Mary was acutely aware of Gabriel standing by her right shoulder. Three times he bent to use both hands on the keyboard to add his own logon again, she felt as if fate was tormenting her. Such an impossible situation, to be physically no more than centimetres from him, to smell his skin and feel the heat of his arm next to her shoulder, it was pure torture.

When it was all done he took a step back. 'And now, the final step. We keep a secure file on the server where we save a specific ID code for each person with access to the high level research files. If someone logs on remotely, say someone's trying to steal data and they have a genuine employee's logon details, they also need that person's unique code phrase to get through to the server. I'm the only one who can access that file with ID phrases. Tell me what yours is going to be and try to make it something nobody else would think of.'

'Six kings of England and one queen,' she said without having to think, because Wendy had warned her to come up with something unique, and this was a phrase from her home life that they never used in front of outsiders, a little joke her dad came out with sometimes, based on the names he had given his children.

'Wow, that was quick! And unusual.' Gabriel chuckled. 'Excellent choice. You must have thought it up in advance.'

When she got up from her chair he took another step back and she looked up into his eyes and said quietly, 'If things had turned out differently I would be able to tell you why I chose that phrase, but no, that's not going to happen. Thank you for helping with this.'

He stared at her for a long moment, and she knew he remembered what he had said to her, that "this was not going to happen". Her calm statement had surprised him, he understood that it was in effect a full stop, dismissing him and making sure he knew she would not approach him again. She hadn't been planning to do this. It was an inspiration born of the moment that surprised her as much as it did him, but now that she had said it she was pleased. There was a tiny change in his stance, as if he had very nearly reached out to touch her, but he controlled himself. 'OK, I'll see you around,' was all he said before he turned and walked away, leaving her standing there feeling desolate and wondering how she had managed to be so cool. It's not the end of it, she consoled herself, that was just the curtain going down on the first act.

20

A week later, after collecting three boxes from Mrs Wong, Mary decided to leave her car on the drive so she could spend the evening in the garage sorting through the boxes of diverse items she had collected so far from Mrs Wong's cluttered house. She unfolded the spare table they sometimes used in the garden, six feet long and the perfect surface to work on. After a few minutes she went back into the house and got her laptop so she could do some research into a few things that might be worth serious money – things Pat had bought in charity shops for a few dollars. She put three ornaments aside to be priced individually and continued to move things into batches and from there into boxes labelled with a set price for anything sold from that particular box. It was the only method she could think of that might streamline the process at the garage sale, but she was fast coming to the conclusion that things weren't moving fast enough. Mrs Wong was not digging deep enough into her chaotic sitting room – she was just picking up small items here and there and at the rate she was going it would be months before they could set a date for the sale, and it might not happen in time for her move to the new, smaller flat.

The next day she called Pat first thing and said in her most decisive voice that they must move faster, and she was coming over after work that afternoon to give her a hand. After her first couple of visits she had realised that Pat was prepared to let her take charge in a way she would never have tolerated from her children, much less from her ex-husband.

'Oh, no, please don't! You're already doing so much for me, I couldn't let you give up your free time, no way!' Pat sounded genuinely embarrassed by Mary's offer, but perhaps there was a vague note of relief behind her protest, as if she was nearly ready to admit that she needed help.

'S-sorry to be so b-bossy, Pat!' Mary tried to sound amused and determined at the same time. 'But I am coming! B-between us we can do it much f-faster. See you at six or so.'

She ended the call with a brief goodbye to avoid any further protests and went to clean her teeth, mentally planning a strategy for how to tackle Pat's living room and decided she must try to dismiss Pat from her mind for the rest of the day.

Hoping to be able to make real progress that night she took the car and stopped at the supermarket on her way to work, put five big cartons on the back seat and continued to the parking building next to Tidewell's. Level 2, she reminded herself as she locked the car and smiled to herself.

Somehow driving up the curved slopes of the ramps made it nearly impossible to automatically estimate which floor she was on and last time she parked there she had searched three levels before she found her car at the end of the day.

That evening when she got out of the lift in the parking building, she caught sight of Gabriel coming through the door from the stairs at the far end. Her feet stopped moving of their own accord and she stood as if frozen, staring down the long aisle between rows of parked cars. He hadn't noticed her and walked towards her looking down at his phone, but at any moment now he would look up. Could she get to her car before him? Quickly she calculated the distance and his pace and decided he would probably be only three or four cars away from hers by the time she got there.

Too close, she told herself, she couldn't deal with him a second time in one day, not after they met in the foyer that morning and he gave her that look that put an emotional barrier between them, as hard to breach as a high stone wall. She turned to the right and walked away at right angles to Gabriel, told herself not to turn her head to see if he had noticed her and proceeded down the length of the parallel row of cars. This way she could walk around the whole floor and by the time she reached her car he would have long gone. But fate was plotting against her because suddenly he was right there after taking a shortcut between cars, and they found themselves face to face, just standing there silently looking at each other.

Before she could move on or say anything Gabriel grabbed her and toppled them both to one side and at the same moment there was an earsplittingly loud crash just beside them. A horrendous blend of breaking glass, crushed plastic and the screech of tortured metal being torn apart. Splinters of glass showered across them; a piece of metal flew through the air and landed just beside them with a clang. Mary lay still, confused and shocked. She looked up into Grabriel's face and said in a trembling voice she didn't recognise as her own, 'You've got glass in your hair.'

'So do you, and a cut on your temple.' He sat up and took her with him, lifted her to sit beside him, and she realised that he must have seen the car coming and lightning fast taken hold of her upper arms and thrown them both to one side, and he was still holding her. Right beside them was a mangled car, its front embedded in the rear of another and its horn blaring. Gabriel got to his feet and pulled her up, looked to see she was steady and dropped his hands. They stared at the wrecked cars, and at the man who had got out of the driver's seat on the far side, who was now standing staring at the mess. The echoing sound of the horn stopped suddenly, and everything seemed deathly quiet apart from a metallic clang when a last piece fell to the floor.

Gabriel took as step closer and studied the man across the roof of the car. 'Are you OK?'

'I'm fine, but only thanks to the airbags going off,' said the man who sounded surprisingly calm, nearly casual. 'I'm sorry I nearly hit you – that was a great save you did, very fast! I don't know what the hell happened.' He shook his head. 'One second I was putting the car into Drive and the next I hit that one at high speed. Is it yours?'

Mary shook her head and Gabriel said, 'No, not ours. Do you need any help? What can I do?'

'I'll call for help. I probably need a roadside rescue truck from my insurance company. And I'll have to report it - don't know whose car I wrecked. Don't worry, I'll deal with it.'

After turning to Mary and looking intently at her face for a long moment, Gabriel took a firm grip on her upper arm and led her away towards the end of the row of cars and she went with him, feeling strangely detached, thinking and reactions suspended. Others were appearing now, clustering around the wrecked cars with loud voices debating if they could or should push the errant car back to where it had been so others could drive out. As they distanced themselves an argument broke out behind them about whether the car should remain where it was until the police arrived or be moved right away. Mary heard the voices and didn't take in a single word, and Gabriel kept her moving forward.

Away from the mayhem Gabriel turned her to face him and said, 'Stand still.' He got a handkerchief out of his pocket and pressed it against her temple and suddenly she swayed on her feet and nearly overbalanced. Since her initial comment about the glass in his hair she had not said a single word since he threw them both to the floor, but now the reality of what she had narrowly escaped suddenly hit her.

She knew she should thank him, but for the moment she was mute, just concentrated on standing straight.

He gave her an assessing look, shoved the handkerchief back in his pocket and said, 'Come here,' and pulled her tight against his chest. And just like he had in the stationery room he slid his hand through her hair and held her against his shoulder. She felt his warm breath on the top of her head.

'I know. That was very scary.' His voice was low and gentle. 'You'll be ok in a moment, it's just the shock. I hope I didn't hurt you when I threw us to the ground.'

She shook her head minutely, leaned into him and closed her eyes. 'Thank you!' she whispered. 'Please, don't let go.'

'I won't.'

They stood there for several minutes, unnoticed by the crowd around the crashed cars, until Mary's mind finally caught up and she moved slightly. He lowered his arms.

'Stand still for a moment.' He started picking shards of glass from her hair, dropping them into the corner. 'The wound on your temple is just a scratch - it's stopped bleeding already. It was lucky it missed your eye. There you are, I think that's all, but perhaps you should brush your hair carefully tonight in case there's more glass hidden in all those curls.'

Before she could think of anything to say he leaned over to one side and brushed his hands roughly through his own hair, and a small shower of glass fell to the floor. 'There!'

Without thinking Mary reached out and put her hand

flat against his shirt. 'You saved me.' She looked seriously into his eyes, still with her hand against his warm chest. 'I know you don't want me, but I love you. I just want you to know that.'

He was about to say something, but she shook her head and walked away with tears pooling in her eyes, trying hard not to cry. Once back at her car she sat for a long time without driving away, trying to imagine what was going through Gabriel's head. Even though she had said that she knew he didn't want her, she knew it wasn't true - he did want her. He just didn't think it would work. What would he have said if she had stayed? she wondered. She shouldn't have said it, and she regretted it now. The hurt she had inflicted on him, not obvious on the surface but she had sensed it. His pain at turning her down more than once, at not being prepared to change his mind. But it was done, and she couldn't do anything about it. She had made her love declaration and now she must move on.

'Thank you, b-but not right now,' said Mary to Pat, who offered her something to eat the moment she opened the front door. 'Let's get started and d-do some work before we sit down and have a coffee or a g-glass of wine.'

Pat was clearly disappointed, but for Mary the last hour had been hard to deal with and now she wanted to get right into something practical and constructive. She gestured at the boxes on the doorstep and Pat moved back into the hallway so she could bring them inside.

Mary piled the boxed against the wall, took the last one in her hand and walked past Pat and into the living room – and nearly screamed in frustration. Now the room was even more chaotic than when she saw it last. Things had been aimlessly moved, and she could picture Pat in here searching for little things to give her on previous trips to collect the boxes. Just moving something off a pile, putting it on top of something else, which would start a land slide, or on the floor where the height of massed things now seemed about to engulf her. One box was the wrong way to start. She returned to the hall and brought the remaining four boxes in a stack, put them in a line on top of what was piled on the floor just inside the door and, ignoring Pat's pleas, started dismantling the first mound close to the boxes.

After watching her for a few minutes Pat joined in and they excavated the mound, layer by layer and put things into boxes. After half an hour it became clear that the five boxes were not enough, so additional little groups of things that related to each other were established along the wall in the hallway.

It's working, thought Mary and smiled at Pat as she returned from depositing yet another few items in the hall. Look at her! She's so pleased.

'There's too much stuff in the hall now,' said Pat after another half hour and frowned at the piles along one wall. 'Any moment now we'll trip on something and break a leg. Let's put some of it on the front porch for now so we have some space to move in and out of the living room.'

They moved out some boxes and two stools that had never been used, which Mary had unearthed from under a pile of linen, and were just about to go back inside when a man hailed them from the flat two doors down in the row.

'Hey, listen!' he called out. 'Is it ok if I come over for a chat?'

Pat said, 'Of course,' and added quietly to Mary. 'He just moved in a few days ago, I've never talked to him.'

'Are you moving in or out?' asked the rotund, middle-aged man as he walked up the path. 'I've just moved in, and if you're getting rid of stuff I'd love to have a look.'

'I'm moving out in a couple of months and sorting out what I can't take with me.' Pat laughed. 'Or let's say, sorting out what I should never have bought in the first place. We're preparing for a garage sale. The new flat is smaller than this one.'

'I'm Douglas, usually called Doug.' He shook hands with them both. 'My wife chucked me out and I've got practically nothing in my kitchen, and very little in the way of bedding, sheets and things. I'd love to have a look at what you're getting rid of.'

An hour later, after calling Archie and telling him she wouldn't be home for dinner, Mary sat at the little kitchen table with Pat and Doug eating soup and toast.

'This has been a godsend,' said Doug. 'I'm so grateful. I'll bring the cash tomorrow or put it into your account, whatever you prefer.' He shook his head and chuckled. 'Just the thought of shopping and trying to work out what I need in the kitchen was driving me crazy, which is why I hadn't done anything about it. I hate shopping. But now I've got practically everything I need apart from a fry pan and a good, sharp knife, so I'm nearly completely set up.'

Mary smiled at the satisfied look on his face and Pat said calmly, 'I've got three fry pans in that cupboard under the sink. And more knives than I need. We'll get them out after we've finished eating.'

When Mary left it was nearly ten o'clock and she realised that she hadn't thought of Gabriel for nearly four hours. Being busy and talking had diverted her and now the satisfaction at how successful their efforts had been made her smile to herself.

'Incredible!' she said to Archie who was sitting at the kitchen table reading with a glass of red wine beside him. 'What we've achieved tonight is borderline miraculous.'

'I saved some food in case you didn't get fed at Mrs Wong's after all. It's on the bench, just pop it in the microwave. And then I want to hear what you did tonight.'

'No, I'll just have a glass of wine while I tell you. We had soup and lots of toast about eight o'clock, I'll have a drink and some crackers.'

She told him the story and ended by describing how much they had put in two big boxes for Doug to carry to his flat before she left. 'So everyone was pleased and lots of stuff disappeared, some of it out of Pat's kitchen cupboards and drawers. Doug got what he needed, including some brand new sheets and a quilt that had never been taken out of its packet. And best of all, having gone through nearly everything in the living room to see what we could find for him, at least we know what's there now and the rest will be much easier.'

21

When Mary's phone signalled a call from Henry in the morning coffee break a couple of weeks later, she didn't take it. She had soon discovered that the conversations in the staff room on the laboratory floor were sometimes as valuable as what she learnt in the labs. She sent him a brief text saying that she'd call back in her lunch hour, put the phone down and returned to the interactions between Bert and the young guy they called Junior.

'Sorry, but it's a definite no,' said Bert decisively and Wendy nodded in agreement. 'Maybe you could do this at home, but in a workplace you're not allowed to decant oxygen like you've suggested we should do, decant it from the big tanks to the handheld ones. I'll tell you why we ...'

'But it would save heaps of money,' interrupted Junior enthusiastically. 'I bet we could spend the savings on better things, and I know how to do it, it's just like topping up a dive tank from a big one on a boat, it's easy. Well, that's compressed air, of course, but the principle is the same. All we need is the double topped gizmo to link them.'

Wendy laughed. 'You're so right about the savings, but we could only do it if we first invested in a room made entirely of concrete with no windows and a steel door or something like it, I imagine - not that I've looked into the specifics. You have no idea yet about the rules that govern what we can and can't do! If you want to find out, you can come and read the policy manuals in my office – that should only take you a week or two.'

Instead of going to the staff room or down to the canteen to have lunch, Mary went outside to the back of the building where one or two people parked their cars. She had seen some staff going in from this side rather than through the front foyer, and when she went to see what was out there, she noticed the little gap between the side of the steps from the door and the wall. A nice little place to sit sheltered from the wind, sunny, and private because of the tall concrete side along the steps. The last time she sat there two people walked up those steps and didn't even look over the side or notice her.

She opened her sandwich parcel, put the phone on her knee and called Henry, and as soon as he answered she pressed the speaker button, so she could eat and talk at the same time. Henry launched straight into question mode like he often did, particularly with her. Ever since she was tiny she had been used to his way of finding things out, to work out what needed to be done and then do it, more so than the others. No wonder he's in the police, she thought now, and prepared herself to cope with what he was bound to ask without revealing too much.

'Why do you think something's wrong?' She tried to sound casual and slightly amused, but in the back of her mind she knew John must had told the others, or at least Henry.

'John said he had a rather strange chat with you last night and asked if I knew anything.'

'Oh, for God's sake! You're not all going to turn up and do another Lintott line-up, are you? Everyone here's been talking about it ever since. The women love it! The sight of the lot of you in a line really turns them on. The CEO told me he keeps watching that video, and his daughter thinks it's wonderful, I bet they all do.' That will distract him, she thought, but no, it had no effect whatsoever.

'But what's wrong, Mopsy? John is concerned it's those shits, who had a bet on you, being a nuisance again. Are they still hassling you?'

'God, no! They wouldn't dare, and now that I'm in the labs I never see even the one who works here.'

'I'll come over after work- it's only an hour's drive. I need to understand what's going on.'

She knew that Henry turning up unexpectedly would make their dad wonder what was going on, too, and then he would worry, and before she knew it the whole lot of them would be discussing it in a group chat on Teams. She had always known that the bond between them and her, even before the abduction, had made them more than siblings. They felt she was nearly like a physical part of each one of them, and if she was hurt they felt the pain, as her dad had said. The only way to de-escalate this was to tell him factually and not get emotional, to make it seem less important than it really was.

'OK, I'll tell you, but just so you know it's not serious enough to panic about. I fell in love with a guy who works here, who's told me he's not for me - that's how he put it - and it's a little bit complicated. But I'll get over it, don't worry.'

'How is it complicated?' asked Henry, inevitably digging down. 'How much do you fancy him?'

'It's not that I just fancy him, not like simple sexual attraction or something. I really, totally love him. He's the most amazing man I've ever met apart from you guys, of course, and I know he's very attracted to me. It's like a forcefield around him, perfectly clear, but he said no, he's not for me, we would both end up hurt. He just walked away when I tried to tell him.' Oh God, she thought and nearly groaned with frustration, now she had told him for too much.

'And you really love him? You sound very serious, Mopsy. I don't think I've ever heard you talk about a guy like this.'

This is what comes of telling your big brothers absolutely everything, she thought, this lack of personal privacy is probably going to continue for the rest of my life, but I can't complain. She smiled to herself - how many women had this kind of support network around them, so much love and protection?

'That's because I've never felt like this about anyone before - not even remotely like this. I'll tell you something that proves how special he is. You know how when I talk to any of you or dad I don't stammer? And then as soon as I talk to someone else, I do? Well, I never stammer when I talk to this guy, never. I can even say words that start with M or P.'

'Oh well, then you'll have to get through to him some way or another, won't you? If you're sure he's into you, too, not just being polite or something. Push him into a corner and make it clear that whatever makes him say it's not going to happen, you can work it out. Do you know what it is – I mean, the reason he says it wouldn't work?'

'Of course I know what it is! He's got this huge scar right down one side of his face, all lumpy and bumpy, and he thinks he'd be too hard to live with, that's what he told me. He's totally convinced he's some kind of monster, it's written all over his otherwise handsome face, and I think he's had years for this totally idiot idea take root and grow in his mind. I bet some stupid girl was nasty about that scar years ago, and it's festered ever since.'

They ended the call when something happened at Henry's end, and Mary was just about to get up when she heard a sound to the far side of her, beyond the little niche she sat in. Instead of getting up as she had been about to, she sat still and hoped whoever it was hadn't been there very long and heard too much. Talking about her problem with Henry without sounding upset had taken a toll, and she needed calm now to settle down, so she could go back upstairs and seem normal.

There was no sound at all now from her left and she heaved a sigh of relief. Whoever that was had not stopped to listen, just walked past and now they were gone.

22

At lunchtime three days after a second highly productive evening at Pat's Mary glanced at a one line message notification on her phone while holding a sticky peanut butter sandwich with one hand and had to put it on her thigh so she could use a clean finger to open the message. This was the first time ever she had received a text message that started with four exclamation points and the fact that it was from Maylene made it even more intriguing. Maylene was sweet and soft spoken, the perfect early childhood teacher, and not inclined to exaggeration or over-the-top reactions and had probably never used an exclamation point in a message ever before.

"!!!! What have you done with my mother? The woman who now lives in her flat is an impostor – an easy-going, cheerful person I have never met before." This was followed by an "I'm laughing until I cry" emoji and another few exclamation points.

Quickly Mary ate the rest of the half-eaten sandwich,

scrunched up her paper bag and went out into the corridor and called Maylene. 'It wasn't m-me,' she said as soon as Maylene took the call. 'I p-promise! She's just changed – nearly overnight. B-but definitely nothing to d-do with me.'

Maylene laughed. 'It's that guy, isn't it? I met him yesterday when I called in to see how she was getting on. Not only is the living room practically cleared out, but she had a guy sitting at the kitchen table with glasses of wine, and they were obviously watching something on his phone and laughing.'

Mary smiled. 'Oh, Doug! D-did she explain who he is?'

'She said he lives two doors down in her row of flats and he's been helping her tidy up! Does he join in when you go over?'

'He's there every evening I think. They g-get along like a house on f-fire. He's been chucked out by his wife and it's one of those friendships that just explode into full b-bloom, no effort involved. Isn't it nice?'

'How old do you think he is? He looks a bit young for her, she's fifty-six, you know.'

'Not too d-different, I don't think,' said Mary who had thought exactly the same thing when she first met Doug. 'He's g-got a twenty-eight year-old daughter who lives in Wellington, and one g-grandchild. I think they're probably much the same age, and it doesn't really matter if they're not, does it?'

They spent another few minutes discussing this surprising development and then Mary noticed the time and ended the call. She herself had been slightly taken aback when she found Doug in Pat's flat the evening after they first met, but it soon became obvious that he enjoyed tidying, sorting and generally getting things organised.

'I'm a freak,' he'd said and grinned at Pat. 'I'm very, very tidy, can't stand a mess. I just go into tidy-up mode at the slightest sight of a mess. No wonder my wife threw me out, I drove her crazy.'

Mary noticed the amused glance Pat directed at him and said, 'And? There's something you're n-not telling me, but clearly Pat knows. What other special talents d-do you have?'

'I'm boring – monumentally and stupendously boring according to my ex-wife, who's just filed a separation request with my lawyer. She claims our marriage stifled her creativity and dulled her down. Her own precise words!'

Pat giggled and Doug turned a smile in her direction. 'But Pat appreciates my talents. So it's a friendship made in heaven – she's made a colossal mess and now I'm helping her tidy up and we have a lot of laughs.'

'And it's lucky that my new flat is just around the corner, so we can continue our Scrabble games any time we like.'

Mary smiled inside at how enjoyable it was to watch this sudden friendship develop and how lovely it was to see Pat so happy and cheerful. Progress was now so rapid that they decided on a date for the garage sale there and then. 'Not that's it's going to involve the garage,' said Pat when they discussed logistics. 'I think having it on my little front lawn would be better providing the weather cooperates.' She gestured at the window. 'Then it's really visible when people drive down the road and we can spread things out.'

23

Three weeks later Mary felt she had perfected the façade she now lived behind, both at work and at home. She had learnt how to hide the hurt and the longing, not to mention the frustration, and though she had private moments when she felt like crying and sometimes did cry, she carried off the pretence better than she had expected to be able to. No pitying glances had come her way from anyone, and she didn't think even the MAMA gang had noticed her hidden sadness.

In the middle of a particularly busy day when Mary had been asked to compare analysis samples in the new advanced software that had just been loaded on the lab computers, something went wrong, and one function she needed came up with a brief notice saying, "this function is not available to this user". She grunted in frustration, logged out of the program and logged back in, hoping that a reset might put it right, but no, the function she needed was still not available. A glance around showed her that the only other two computers, which had the new software she needed, were in use.

She went in search of Wendy, who was the person who saw to it that everyone was busy with relevant things and had what they needed. 'It isn't working, I can't d-do the c-comparison,' said Mary, breathless after hurrying around the entire floor trying to locate Wendy. 'All it says is t-that the f-function I need isn't available to me.'

'Oh, bugger!' exclaimed Wendy. 'I really need that done today. Maybe you'll have to wait for Dion to finish what he's doing on my computer and do it there, no, wait, that won't work. I need him to do those graphs, too. And it would happen today of all days!'

Concerned Mary watched the usually composed and smiling Wendy look as if she was about to tear her hair out. 'Can't we just g-get someone f-from IT to fix it?'

'This is so new,' said Wendy, visibly trying to slow down and collect herself, but clearly worried. 'When Gabriel came and set it up on those three machines the other day, he warned me that it was tricky software, but it seemed very clever and now we've uploaded all the data to it. I'm not sure if his second-in-command in IT, what's his name – Angus - is quite up to dealing with this.'

'Where is Gabriel? Is he on l-leave?'

'He's in hospital. He got a terrible bout of that new strain of flu, and it went to his lungs, and he got double-sided pneumonia. Bert went to see him and said it was terrible to see a big, strong guy like that lying there helpless, really ill. I'll call Angus and see if he can check it out.

When Angus appeared he seemed confident that he

would be able to sort out whatever had gone wrong. 'Let's have a go,' he said when he sat down in front of Mary's computer. 'I've read up on this since we bought it, so maybe I can do it. As my mum says whenever I say something can't be done, "it can't be that hard, can it?" And she's usually right.'

He grinned at Wendy, who looked doubtful. 'I'm not going to break it, don't worry - I'll just have a look at some settings. If it's working on the other two computers Gab loaded it on, then it's got to be in the settings for this particular logon.'

Wendy smiled and still not looking very hopeful left them to it, so Mary took the opportunity she had been waiting for. 'How is Gabriel g-getting on? Is he improving?'

'I went up to the hospital last night after work, but he was nearly asleep. He had an oxygen mask on, and they wouldn't let him take it off so he could talk. Well, the nurse said he's not allowed to talk at the moment, not until his breathing improves a bit more, but she said he's definitely on the mend.'

'Was his f-family there?' She tried to stop herself, but she simply couldn't. She had to know, make sure someone looked after his interests and took care of whatever needed doing.

'No, they live overseas, he told me a few weeks ago when his dad called from Wales. His dad's got some kind of science job there at a university, and Gab hasn't any siblings. I did tell him last night that I could call his parents and let them know, and he got really agitated, shook his head and tried to say no. I could hear it through the mask, so I said

OK, I won't do it. And if he's getting better there's probably no need to worry them.'

He thought for a moment with creases between his eyebrows. 'And if he gets worse I'm sure the hospital knows who he's listed as his next of kin, someone a bit closer, cousins or something.'

He swung back to the screen, and Mary watched fascinated as he moved from one thing to another, totally focused and leaning forward as if he had to be as close to the screen as possible. After a surprisingly short time he got up and gestured towards the chair, 'It's all yours, just a setting that hadn't clicked in for some reason. Got to go, with Gab away I'm the only person here who's competent to help people with stuff like this.'

Mary spent the afternoon in a quandary. Should she take the risk of finding out more, or would it seem intrusive? Did she dare go to the hospital and visit him? And then just after five, when her dad sent a text message to remind her he was going out for dinner with a former colleague who had just retired, she took her courage in both hands and caught a bus to the hospital. Standing in front of the big display in the main entrance she read right through the explanations of what was on the five levels and decided that someone with pneumonia would be in one of the three medical wards on Level 2. A few minutes later a woman at the reception desk told her that Gabriel was in room 14 in Ward 2. Mary took a deep breath, squared her shoulders, as she always did when faced with a challenge, and walked through the swing doors to Ward 2.

The door to room 14 was closed and there was only one name in the little card holder beside the door. A single room, she thought, instantly alarmed. Did it mean that he was in real danger? She knocked gently, but there was no response, so she opened the door and stood with her hand on the doorhandle, ready to turn on her heel and leave if there were nurses or doctors in there doing something to him. But the room was quiet and still, a blind was pulled down to screen out the slanting evening sunlight, and Gabriel lay on his back like an effigy with his arms down his sides on top of the sheet, the head part of his bed slightly raised. His face was covered in beard stubble, and there was no oxygen mask over his mouth – he was deeply asleep. She turned around, closed the door again and went to find someone who could answer questions.

'Yeah, he's improving,' said the young doctor she found talking to a nurse further down the corridor. 'He's doing quite well all things considered, but we'll have to keep him here for a few more days. He lives alone, so we can't send him home just yet, worse luck. We're desperately short of beds right now.'

'I m-might be able to organise that,' said Mary recklessly. 'When can he be m-moved?'

'Oh, tomorrow I'd think – if he continues to improve at the rate he is now, or the next day. He's doing really well.'

'OK, l-let me check a few things f-first, and then I'll c-come back and t-talk to you in the morning. He can p-probably stay with my dad. He's good at l-looking after people, brought up a whole c-crowd of us. He's retired now and he has p-plenty of room.'

She returned to room 14 and went inside, gently closed the door and studied Gabriel, who was still asleep and looked exhausted. She didn't want to risk waking him, but she wanted to be close to him for a while, so she moved the chair from the corner and sat down at right angles to the bed. Quietly watching his chest rise and fall she felt tears pool in her eyes. To see him so helpless looking, so tired and ill, was heartbreaking. She remembered the feel of his arms around her and the strength of him, and the contrast made her heart clench. She leaned forward and curled her fingers around his hand and let their joined hands rest on his chest. The feel of his skin made her smile despite her tension.

She closed her eyes for a moment and relived the moment in the stationery room when he ran his hand up through her hair and clasped her head to hold her against him and she absorbed his smell. But within seconds she opened her eyes and told herself off for being silly. She mustn't get her hopes up, this would change nothing from his point of view apart from possibly make him angry. Sitting there holding his hand she thought of how she could turn the impulsive plan she had put to the doctor into reality. She left ten minutes later, after first bending over Gabriel to run a finger down along the scar from his temple nearly to his jaw before she lifted his hand, kissed his knuckles and put his hand back on the sheet. Turning to leave she stopped and looked down at him and on an impulse she got the stone coin out. She brushed Gabriel's thick brown hair from his forehead with gentle fingers and put the stone coin just above his left eyebrow. She whispered, 'I love you,' and ran a finger along his eyebrow, before she picked up the stone again, slid it back into her pocket and left.

Lying still with his eyes closed, Gabriel listened to the door softly closing before he let his eyelids lift. He had known who was holding his hand from the moment he woke up, and he had managed to not open his eyes by sheer willpower. He felt incapable of dealing with any kind of conversation with Mary while he was so tired. Saying no on previous occasions had taken a toll on his resolution, the most difficult decision he had ever made about a woman, but right now it might be beyond him. Only the thought that he was protecting them both from future hurt had stopped him opening his eyes. The way Mary had quietly and decisively dismissed him that day when he set her up with the lab software, that had surprised him and though it had fitted with his own decision, it had still been devastating, and it still was, particularly when she told him she loved him after the parking building incident. But now, lying there in a hospital bed, tired and still unwell, he admitted to himself that her touch just now had nearly made him sit up and grab hold of her, to never let her go.

On the way out Mary stopped at the nurses' office and asked to speak to whoever was in charge of the ward. 'I know he's not g-got f-family in New Zealand,' she said to the nurse who came out to speak to her. 'And I know t-two guys from work have been to see him, but has anybody else v-visited him?'

'Not that I know of, and the first three days after he was admitted he wasn't allowed anyone in his room without our permission, so I wouldn't think so. I've been on the afternoon to evening shift all week, and I haven't seen anyone coming – apart from two men, as you say.'

'If I c-come b-back tomorrow m-morning to tell him he can stay with m-my dad – to f-free up a bed f-for you. Will I be able to g-get into the ward?'

'Just press the call button on the wall beside the doors and someone will come to see what you want. I'm not on in the morning, but I'll leave a note for them to let you in. The promise of a bed freed up will work magic.'

Today is Thursday, thought Mary on the bus ride home, which involved two changes of bus and a wait at each stop. I'll call in and tell Gretchen I'll be slightly late tomorrow morning, but I won't talk directly to Wendy in case she asks me why. Maybe I could say I've got to take dad to the doctor, or that I have an appointment I forgot about. But I have to go back to see him before I bring dad with me to take him home.'

24

Sitting in the corner of the sofa in the living room, Mary pondered the options and tried to make solid plans for the next day while she waited for her father to come home from his dinner out. She sent an email to Gretchen at work and asked her to tell Wendy that she would be a couple of hours late the next day, but she would be happy stay and catch up after five. After some thought she used the vague excuse of "an appointment I forgot to mention earlier" without specifying what it was about. The next step was to decide on an approach for her visit to Gabriel to convince him to do what she wanted. Having experienced his unconditional "no" on two occasions she knew it was crucial to get this right at the outset, to leave no little loophole for him to bring out that uncompromising "no" response. After vacillating between various options, some of which seemed too weak and others too open to debate, she suddenly knew what she must do.

Smiling to herself, she went to make a couple of cheese

sandwiches with pickles to have instead of the dinner she never got around to cooking, having been too immersed in her plans and ideas and returned to the sofa with a plate just as she heard her father's key in the door.

'Are you having a late snack or is that your dinner?' said her dad when he saw her with the sandwich in her hand. 'Steve said to say hi to you and tell you he saw the Lintott line-up on Instagram. He was very impressed.'

'Listen dad, I've got a little problem, and you might say no, but I want to help this guy from work. He's the IT specialist and he's in hospital after a terrible dose of that flu strain that wasn't in the latest vaccine, and it turned to pneumonia. He's got no family here, and the hospital is desperately short of beds, but they won't let him go home to live on his own until he's fully recovered.'

'The poor guy! Is he a special friend of yours? And what is it they think might happen if he goes back to his place?'

'I didn't ask, the doctor just said they'll have to keep him in for another three or four days if there's nobody he can stay with. But would you mind if he came and stayed here for those few days, just until he's back on his feet? I don't think you'd have to do anything for him. It's not as if he's in a wheelchair or anything, it's just that he's got to be in a place where there's someone else around some of the time.'

'I don't mind,' said her dad. 'He can have Henry's room, it's nice and bright and there's an armchair in there now, which kind of makes it like a little sitting room, and there's the new bathroom between that room and yours.'

He paused and frowned. 'But you'll probably prefer that he doesn't use that – it's your bathroom now apart from when the boys come home.'

'I'll use yours while he's here, so he can have that one to himself. I'm going to pop in to see him tomorrow morning, and then I'll let you know when you can pick him up, if that's ok with you, but it might not be tomorrow, depends on how he's getting on. But even if it's on Saturday maybe you can do it, because I've got Pat's garage sale and I have to be there to help her.'

'No problem, 'said her dad and got to his feet. 'Look, I'm going to bed now, don't sit up all night. Oh, what's this guy's name?'

'Gabriel. And, of course, this plan might not work. He's as stubborn as a pig and he's bound to think he doesn't need any help, so I'll have to get around that, one way or another. But I'll message you tomorrow when I've seen him and the doctor and tell you if I managed. Goodnight!'

This calm acceptance of having a stranger come and recuperate with them surprised Mary. Not that her dad wasn't hospitable and friendly, but that he'd asked no further questions surprised her. She had already constructed an excuse for why she had gone to the hospital and interviewed Gabriel's doctor, had it all ready to trot out when he asked, but he didn't. He just said it was fine and didn't ask a single thing after that loosely phrased "is he a special friend of yours". But their slightly unexpected conversation was not important, what mattered was providing Gabriel with a safe and comfortable place to stay so he didn't have to stay in hospital.

She went to bed thinking about the next morning and how she planned to get Gabriel to agree and nearly laughed out loud as she pictured the scene. Inspiration had struck not long before her dad returned, just when she had decided she'd have to wing it and maybe fail when she talked to Gabriel. But now she knew what she would do, and it made her smile in the dark. She wondered if the videos were still on someone's hard drive. Long ago all her brothers had filmed her bossing one of the others around, and she felt sure there was a whole collection on someone's laptop. They used to show her sometimes when she was younger and laugh with her at how funny she had been.

One in particular came back to her now and made her giggle. She must have been five or maybe a bit younger and dead set on forcing Henry to drive her somewhere she wanted to go. The video showed her following him around, saying 'You *have* to! Don't you *understand*? If you don't I'll never get to see it! Stop walking away and *listen* to me!' while he continued to walk away. Next she turned up with the little red stool she used to stand on to help at the kitchen bench and tried to get in front of Henry's legs, clearly intent on climbing up to make her demand a bit more face-to-face. But Henry evaded her, just walked around her and she never realised at the time that he did it on purpose to make the video better. The final scene had her with her arms and legs wound tight around Henry's lower legs shouting up at him, 'You have to, it's the *law* – you *have* to obey me, Henry, I'm a queen.'

That stroppy little voice, thought Mary, maybe I can be just as bossy now, if he tries to resist. I bet I can be just as over the top assertive as I was then, and I'll use that voice – and take him completely by surprise. Thank God, I don't stammer when I talk to him, or I couldn't do it.

And as is often the case with problems we think about last thing before going to sleep, a further refinement developed in her sleeping mind. At half past six the next morning Mary called John and said as soon as he replied, 'Hey, John – can I take your name in vain in a good cause, in case I need some extra ammunition? Just to help me with a little project I'm launching today?'

After considering how to make her request sound as if she was not talking about Gabriel, she decided to make it sound as if it was someone on her lab team, someone she wanted to help and hopefully he would assume it was a woman.

There was a longish silence at the other end before he replied. 'Hmm – I think you need to tell me a bit more, Mopsy. What's the project and why would my name help?'

'Someone who's been really useful to me since I moved to the labs is in hospital and this is what's going on ...'

She related the whole story without mentioning Gabriel's name and managed to avoid using any gender specific pronouns. She talked about the illness, the problem of liberating a bed for someone else because "going back to an empty flat would be potentially dangerous".

'Apparently double-sided pneumonia takes a bit of time to get over,' she said casually. 'And dad's ok with having a house guest for a few days.'

She held her breath when she finished her explanation, and John laughed quietly and said casually, 'So you fell in love with my old mate Gab, and he's been holding you at arm's length?'

Embarrassed and indignant at the same time, Mary exclaimed, 'You guys are like a gossip network in six dimensions! I bet Henry told you about our talk the other day and you put two and two together, ha? And you linked it to Gabriel calling you so you could organise the Lintott line-up. Can't I have any secrets?'

'Don't get upset, Mopsy, you know I'm always on your side. And of course I worked it out – I'm a detective, aren't I? I could tell from your voice when we talked about him before, after the line-up, that something emotional was linked to this. And then Henry said he was a bit concerned about how serious you sounded, so when he mentioned the scar you told him about it was obvious. But listen, I'm on your side, as I said. I'll tell you a bit more if you let me go and get dressed now. I'd just come out of the shower when you called, and air drying is making me cold.'

Five minutes later he called back. 'OK, I'll tell you this if you promise not to quote what I'm going to tell you to Gabriel. He'd feel like his privacy was being violated if he found out. What you said to Henry about some idiot woman making out nobody could live with him because he looks like a monster was spot on. It happened exactly like that - and to top it off, publicly.'

'Oh, God, that's awful, but how did you find out?'

'Oh, just coincidence – I was having a drink with another Rugby mate of ours recently, and I mentioned how Gab had contacted me and what we did about those little shits who were stalking you at work, and Buster – that's they guy I was talking to – he told me about this woman who posted something really nasty about Gab on social media – with a photo of him! Some years ago now, but he heard about it or saw it, and it must have stuck. Imagine how humiliated and hurt he must have been. So whatever you're going to do, you can refer to me, so long as you don't push him too hard.'

'I promise!' she said with her fingers crossed, because what he considered "too hard" might be very different from her idea.

25

It worked perfectly, just as yesterday's nurse had promised. Mary was admitted to the ward a few minutes after pressing the button beside the door. 'Any news?' she asked the nurse, a male one today, who let her in. 'Has a d-doctor seen him today?'

'They've just done a discharge round, and the doctor said he can go home today provided he has company at home for a few days. We've asked the pharmacy to send up the antibiotics they want him to take for another week, just to make sure we've knocked this thing dead – the pneumonia, I mean.'

He gave her a cautious look, hesitated and said, 'But this is where it gets a bit complicated. Now he says he'll discharge himself at his own risk and go straight back to his empty house or wherever he lives, whether we approve or not, which is not a good thing. We can't stop him - he's got the right to do it if he signs a disclaimer saying he understands the risks.'

This needed no thought at all as far as Mary was concerned. Clearly she wasn't going to let this mad idea go ahead. 'Listen,' she said in a low voice, reluctant to be overheard by anyone else. 'I think I can f-fix this. I'll go and see him now, so p-please keep everyone out of his room until I've knocked this stupid idea out of him and g-got him to see reason. My dad will p-pick him up any time I t-text him – I just need a bit of t-time to convince Gabriel. Maybe half an hour.'

The door to Gabriel's room was open, and she saw the end of the bed without going in, he was sitting up today. After a moment of concentration she knew she had her four year-old persona right there at the front of her mind, ready to pull out when needed, and walked into the room closing the door behind her.

'What are you doing here?' Gabriel stared at her, suspicious and irritated in equal parts. 'How did you get in at this time of the day?'

'Special powers of persuasion and a bit of blatant bribery,' said Mary and sat down on the edge of the bed. 'Now listen to me, and don't interrupt until you've heard what I'm going to say. It's my turn to use that unconditional no, so just hold your horses until I've finished. No way can I let you go home to an empty place and risk getting sick again. You saved me and now it's my turn.'

She took hold of his hand and curled her fingers tight

around his, ignored his attempt to free his hand and continued quickly, as if she hadn't noticed. 'My dad lives in a huge house full of unoccupied bedrooms and he's expecting you to come and stay for a few days. You can have your own bathroom and do whatever you like. He won't bother you, but he's good company, very clever and funny. He'll be here in a couple of hours. He can do one of two things - it's up to you. Either he drives you to your place to pick up some clothes and whatever you need, or you just use what you can find in all the wardrobes in the house, stuff my brothers leave behind now and then as they come and go. At least three of them are as big as you are.'

She had no intention of telling him that she still lived at home, or her plan might fail. He was just about to open his mouth and say that non-negotiable no of his, she could see that determined look coming, so she got to her feet and changed to little Bossy Mopsy.

'You *have to* – if you don't I'll scream and scream and the police will come, and they'll put you in prison for being mean to me. It's the *law*. You *have* to do what I say.' She stamped her foot and glowered at him. He was stunned and his expression made her laugh. Then his hand relaxed in hers and suddenly he was laughing too.

'Come closer and bend down, you little terror!' he said, but she pulled her hand away and remained on her feet. 'So you can smack me for being bossy? No way!'

And then something changed, she felt it like a physical sensation. Something in him let go and tears pooled in her eyes. 'Please?' she said quietly. '*Please* say you will, or I'll worry day and night, and I'll probably park outside your place and sit there at night just to see lights go on and off, so I know you're alive.' Her voice broke on a little sob. '*Please* don't make this any harder.'

'I won't fight you - and thank you. I think you could persuade me to do nearly anything.'

Mary laughed. 'Don't tempt me!' She saw the flash of desire on his face as clearly as if he had told her what her reply made him think of, so she gave him a sly smile to make sure he knew she had noticed.

'What's your father's name?'

'Arthur Lintott, always called Archie, He's just turned seventy-five, he's a retired schoolteacher – science and maths - and he loves crime dramas, cryptic crosswords and sport. I'll call him as I leave. I'm sure the staff want me out of here.'

He reached for her hand and held it tight, and she smiled; a first physical touch initiated by him since he held her after the out of control car nearly hit them, and it made her heart swell with happiness. 'How did you persuade them to let you in this early? Did you throw a tantrum and threaten them with prison?'

'Don't be silly! I just said I was going to liberate a bed for them, and they were so grateful they let me in.'

She bent forward, ran a finger along his scar and kissed his cheek, then she walked out the door to find the nurse she had talked to earlier.

'Hi, dad,' she wrote in the email app on her phone ten minutes later at the bus stop, having decided that what she needed to say was too long for a text message. 'Gabriel is happy to stay for a few days, so you can pick him up before lunch. They're waiting for some drugs he supposed to take to come up from the pharmacy, and they want him to have a shower, so if you time it for half past ten or eleven it should work well. They want to get rid of him before midday, so they can get the room cleaned and ready for the next patient. He's in room 14 in medical ward 2. I might be late home, but I'll buy pizza from the Italian place on my way home, so don't cook anything. I made the bed in Henry's room this morning, and I think we can both use the bathroom at that end, so I've not bothered to move my stuff.'

Trying to predict how Gabriel would react when he discovered she lived at home with her father was not easy. He had given up on the resistance, but it might reappear when he found out she had deceived him and that she still lived at home. But it wasn't deception, she told herself, she had just said that her dad lived in a huge house, which was perfectly true, if not the whole truth. She would pretend she hadn't realised how she put it and say he just took it wrong, if he mentioned it. On the other hand, the way he had smiled and called her a little terror was a good sign, so maybe he was over this "I'm a monster and nobody could stand living with me" thing. But these intermittent musings became less frequent as the day wore on. And then she didn't think about it at all when one of the other lab technicians suddenly declared he was going to be sick, made a dash for the toilets and then went home.

'Thank goodness we've got you!' said Bert and ran a hand through his unruly hair, which already looked as if he'd done it several times since that morning. 'Wendy says you're very quick, so let's see if we can complete this sequence before the end of the day even without Alan.'

26

When Mary walked in the front door at quarter to seven with two pizza boxes balanced on one hand she heard Gabriel and her father laughing in the kitchen-cum-living room and found them sitting side by side on the sofa watching videos of herself as a tiny girl, bossing her big brothers around, and they were laughing so hard they hadn't heard her come in. She stood there for a few moments and tried to understand how those videos could be played on the TV, then she walked around the sofa and stopped in front of them, taking them totally by surprise.

'So this is what goes on when I'm out working and earning money to buy you pizzas,' she said mock-accusingly. 'How are you feeling, Gabriel? You look a lot better than you did this morning.'

He grinned. 'If I looked a bit weak and feeble then, it was probably because I was terrified – lying in a hospital bed being threatened with police and prison was scary. But

Archie tells me threatening people with prison is a habit of yours and he'll protect me.'

'Ha! Don't forget I've got two brothers and one sister-in-law who are police officers. Well, I'll go and dish up pizza, so we can eat while these are still warm.'

They ate pizza right there rather than at the kitchen table, with a roll of paper towels handy and glasses of red wine, cosy and relaxed. Mary glanced sideways at Gabriel now and then, amazed at how he and her dad had become such good friends in just a few hours. Mind you, her dad was hard to resist, charming and easy-going and interested in nearly everything, and those videos would have made it easier.

'I didn't know we still had those videos,' she said after a while. 'Or that you could watch them on the TV. I thought they were long gone, or maybe on someone's hard drive on a laptop or something. I remember William showing them to me years ago - we used to watch them together and laugh at how I tried to make all those big guys do what I wanted. I think they were on disks at that stage, but we don't even have a disk player now, do we?'

'It's one of the advantages of having a house guest who's an IT specialist. Very handy!' Her father laughed. 'When Gabriel told me about your tantrum in his hospital room this morning, I said I must see if I can do something with those videos of you – this was on the way to his flat – so he brought some equipment over and sorted it out once we got here. And now those videos are on the hard drive on my laptop, and I can channel them to the TV.'

'And they're also on an external hard drive,' said

Gabriel. 'For you or your brothers. Definitely worth making sure they don't end up lost and forgotten. I haven't laughed so much in years.'

'What a useful guy you are!' Mary reached for another slice of pizza with anchovies, her favourite kind, and tried to imagine these two in her dad's car.

How had that conversation about her tantrum started? Had Gabriel said, 'Hey, let me tell you how your daughter gets her way, even when someone says no.' Or had her dad found something out from John or Henry. As far as her happiness and safety were concerned there were no boundaries in this family, so he might know a whole lot more than what she had told him when she asked if Gabriel could come and stay. Or had her dad asked how she had persuaded him, or worse, why he had initially refused? She hoped nothing had been said about the stationery room, not because there was anything bad or embarrassing about it, but in her mind it had become a deeply personal and significant incident, something she often thought about last thing at night before she dropped off to sleep and sometimes dreamed about.

When they went to bed she hugged her father like she always did, walked further down the long hallway with Gabriel and stopped by his door.

'Good night! You can have the bathroom first, I've got some things I want to sort out on my laptop, so I'm not ready to go to bed yet. The towels on the rail under the window are yours. And if you sleep in, I might not see you in the morning. I have to go and help a friend's mother hold a gigantic garage sale.'

She half turned to continue to her room and ignored the little movement of his hand, as if he had once again stopped himself from reaching out and touching her. This is not the time, she thought, I still feel very uncertain about this situation. God knows what he and dad talked about. If John came up in the conversation and dad messaged John, then Gabriel might know far too much, and he'll realise we've talked about him.

27

Sitting on her bed in her usual nightwear of T-shirt and panties, Mary spent an hour alternately reading and thinking and maybe hoping just a tiny bit that Gabriel would knock on her door. But of course he wouldn't do that, the idea was ridiculous. Why would he, when she had adopted that cool stance when they said good night in the hallway? After all the pushing and persuading she had done to date, she must step back now and leave the initiative to him. But telling herself that she was a fool didn't stop her longing and wishing things hadn't become so complicated.

When Mary came out of the bathroom just before midnight she saw that the door to Gabriel's room was not quite closed, and the light was still on. He might have fallen asleep with it on, of course, or he might be reading or, the worst scenario, he might be feeling unwell. Maybe leaping straight back into normal life and having wine and pizza had been too much and too soon. She stood in the hallway considering whether she should do something, intervene in some way or simply ignore it and go to bed. But she had to admit to herself that if she went to bed, she would be unable to go to sleep with those questions churning around in her mind, so she knocked very softly so as not to wake him up if he had fallen asleep.

'Yes?' His voice was quiet, but he didn't sound as if she had woken him up. She pushed the door a little, so she could look in. 'Are you OK? I saw your light on, do you need something?'

Gabriel was sitting up with a book on his knees. 'Well ...' he said slowly. 'If you wouldn't mind, yes, I ...'

'Oh God, you're not feeling worse, are you?' she pushed the door fully open and took a quick step inside. 'Tell me what's wrong, what do you need?'

'I need you to come right in and close the door,' said Gabriel coolly. 'And then come and give me a hug, perhaps? Or just climb in with me and I'll give you a hug.'

Was he serious? There was a look of nearly hidden amusement on his face, but even so she hesitated for a few moments. Gabriel folded the quilt back. 'Well, are you coming? You can't stand there all night dressed like that, you little terror. What if someone comes in?'

Mary took two slow steps closer, and Gabriel grinned. 'Are you worried about climbing in with me while your dad's sleeping a couple of doors down? I'm only going to hug you, Mopsy. I don't have the strength for anything loud and energetic right now. But perhaps you should close the door?'

Suddenly she laughed, turned to close the door and said mockingly, 'You're sure? Is this really going to happen? You really want this? No more of that unconditional "no" that was driving me mad?'

She got into the bed beside him, while he put his book to one side, slid down and turned on his side so their faces were very close. She raised her hand and once again ran her finger down the scar on his cheek. 'How did you get this?'

'I got flicked by the end of a steel cable that snapped. Someone was towing a big trailer with a boat on it up a ramp down by the fishing club and I was just walking past. The cable snapped where it was attached to the trailer, and it flicked out in a half circle and hit my face.'

'How old were you?'

'Fifteen. A bad age for something like that to happen. I've got that funny skin that heals in lumps. But I was lucky it didn't take my eye out.'

'Why do you always say ...' She stopped. This was not the right time to ask those difficult questions like the one about "I would be too hard to live with" - it could wait for another day. But Gabriel pulled her close and kissed her forehead. 'There's no need to worry. I think I've been snapped out of what you called the "monster face thing". I heard you talking one day outside the back door at work. I worked out you must have been sitting in that little corner beside the steps.'

'Aha, it was you who walked past! I thought someone had, but then I decided I'd been mistaken.' She thought for a moment and decided he needed to understand that she hadn't just idly gossiped about him. 'I was talking to Henry, I think, but I also talked to John about you, because I was beside myself with frustration. I knew you belonged to me, it wasn't just a selfish wish, it was something I'd felt inside me ever since we got locked in the stationery room. Such a strong feeling right from the start, I couldn't reason myself out of it. Not that I wanted to.' She kissed his chin. 'What else do you know that I'm not aware of?'

He tightened his arms and rolled on his back, and she found herself enveloped in a tight hug. 'I woke up when you came to the hospital the first time,' he said quietly. 'That's what changed everything. Somehow I managed to keep my eyes shut – self-protection again – but I heard what you said, and I felt your fingers running along my scar and then you put something warm on my forehead. What was it?'

She tilted her head up at an angle and smiled. 'It was the stone coin. I got it out from my bra, which is where I keep it if I don't have any pockets. I've carried it all the time since you gave it to me, just in case it really is magical, hoping it will bring you to me. I put it on your forehead, hoping it would do something – I've no idea what I was hoping for, it just seemed the right thing to do, maybe it would work some the magic.'

'Really?' Gabriel chuckled. 'Is that a science thing you learnt at university? Good thing I didn't know it had come straight from your bra at the time, or my eyes would have opened immediately and spoilt the whole thing.'

Mary pushed her face against his neck and sighed. 'I'm

so happy now,' she mumbled and revelled in the feeling of her lips moving against his skin. 'This is where I belong. This is bliss after all the weeks of frustrations and feeling rejected and hurt. You're my safe place.'

'I'll do everything I can to keep you safe, always.'

'What would you do if I hurt myself?

'Hug you – but I'd staunch the blood flow first, of course.'

'And if I just cried for no reason?'

He pulled back a little so he could see her face and the look he slanted at her made her smile. 'I'd hug you of course. Isn't that the universal comfort thing?'

'Have you hugged a lot of people? You're so good at it - outstanding actually, so you must have had a lot of practice.' She knew this question would probably open Pandora's box and make for an uncomfortable conversation, but she wanted him to get used to being open with her.

Seemingly unfazed, he said casually, 'God, no! Before that day in the stationery room I hadn't hugged anyone for years. I don't have anyone to hug, you must know that by now. And then I didn't hug anyone until that day in the park when you asked me to hold you. That hug did something to me.'

She knew he hadn't meant what had just flicked into her head, but she said it anyway. 'I know, I could feel that it did something to you.'

He chuckled quietly and she kissed the side of his jaw, which was about the full extent of her reach when he held her like this. 'Well, this is your new normal, then. Your life will be full of hugs from now.'

They went to sleep like that and when Mary woke at dawn, Gabriel was still deeply asleep, so she crept out of his room and went to check the medicine bottle she had spotted on the kitchen table the previous night. Twice a day with food, she read on the label, put it down and went back to Gabriel's room. As soon as she slid into bed beside him he woke up.

'I was dreaming,' he said and reached to pull her closer. 'I had this strange dream that we were moving into a house, and I was installing those little nightlights in every room, like in this house – the ones that come on automatically when it starts getting dark.'

She couldn't believe he was talking about a house already. As if plans and ideas had been forming in the back of his head all that time while he was busy fending her off and telling her they would never be together. He couldn't have given her a better confirmation about how serious he was.

'Of course, we'll have them everywhere. My family first put them in all the wall sockets when I was found and they realised that the dark traumatised me, but those weren't automatic, someone had to go around and switch them on every evening.' She giggled. 'And then I started wandering around and turning them back on in the mornings after dad had turned them off, and nobody noticed they were on while it was daylight, not until it started getting dark, so then they left them on all the time. When I first started turning them back on I used to count them to make sure I'd remembered them all on and not left one out – there were fourteen – it was so important. And then a few years later they were replaced with those that come on by themselves at dusk, they're much better.'

'We'll have lots of them,' said Gabriel. 'As many as you like.'

And she said out of pure mischief, 'Or maybe we should just add another bathroom or two and live here with dad?'

There was a pause, during which Mary, inwardly cringing, tried to think of how to say, "I'm just kidding" and make it sound convincing, but before she had managed to get it out, Gabriel started to laugh. 'You won't believe this, but that's exactly what Archie said when I told him the truth about us.'

Outraged, she exclaimed, 'The truth? Which part of it?'

She felt his chest vibrating with laughter and realised he was thoroughly enjoying this, an unexpected trait. Somehow she had never imagined that he would enjoy playing this kind of game. 'Oh, this and that,' he said casually. 'You know, how you came after me and told me I was yours, that I belonged to you - and how I told you it could never happen. And that you told me the details about the abduction and how you developed this sixth sense that allows you to identify men in the dark by the way their skin smells, which now includes me.'

She couldn't believe it. In six or so hours her father and Gabriel had told each other everything by the sound of it, but this comment about the house was astounding. Or was he teasing? She was beginning to realise that teasing was a talent of his, suppressed until now and very enjoyable, but something she must quickly learn to deal with because he concealed it so well, or she would forever be taken in.

'You're joking, aren't you? I mean, about living here?'

'Sorry, can I rewind and start again, please? I jumped the gun there, which was stupid. This is how it developed. I told Archie there's nothing in the whole world I want more than being with you, but first I must find a bigger flat. My rented flat is the size of a shoe box. Not because I can't afford it, and I'm planning to buy a nice apartment as soon as I find a good one – it's just that I haven't found one I like yet. I probably haven't spent enough time looking. And Archie said that thing about living here. It's not a conspiracy, Mopsy – don't panic.'

A series of potential problems presented themselves and made Mary mute for a few moments. 'But, the boys,' she said finally, 'and their partners and kids. They come back all the time, and we celebrate various birthdays and holidays together, and the house is full to bursting point. You haven't taken in the complications! This isn't your average family in any respect. So many of us and how we stick together. And when they come, they stay here in this house. We're more like a tribe than a family - multi-generational and constantly spreading. You probably wouldn't be able to live with all the mad stuff that goes on in this house.'

'But you run the whole family, don't you? Archie said

you organise all those things, so who would do it if you're not living here? And he told me about your system for getting all the beds changed after big family events, and how you two go that laundromat. You have an amazing talent for organising things. It just wouldn't be the same if we don't live here. He told me about cricket in the garden, and kitchen chaos, and how everyone ends up with little kids getting up and moving into someone else's bed in the middle of the night. It sounds wonderful to me.'

'You haven't thought it through,' she said calmly, determined to make him see all the snags he had not thought of yet. 'Where would we be with your friends when they pop in for a beer or whatever they do? And your parents when they return? It would be like you don't have a place of your own, and after a while you would want more ... privacy or independence or whatever you want to call it. And then you might resent it.'

'Oh, I don't think so. I was actually sitting here thinking about it, picturing in my mind, when you came in last night. I was imagining how to make it work. When Archie said it, I thought he was joking, but he wasn't, he was deadly serious, but then he changed his mind, or he pretended to. And he said, no, he'd sell this house and buy a smaller one, and there was no need for me to worry about his crazy family. And as I sat here tonight, after you said good night and went to your room, I was unable to stop thinking about it, and I realised it's perfect. He wouldn't be living alone and this place, which is the centre of your ever expanding tribe, would continue to be the place where everyone gathers. Where else would that happen? All it needs is another bathroom or two and a couple of bedrooms added, or a little free standing house in the corner of the garden. And there's plenty of room out the back, even when you consider the need for space to play cricket. The garden is huge, so there's ample room to build a bit more accommodation, which I would obviously pay for instead of buying an apartment.'

'For us?' she asked and realised her voice was trembling. 'A little house for us?'

He held her tighter. 'Perhaps a little place for us, but not a full-scale thing with a kitchen and all that. Just a bedroom and a bathroom, perhaps a bedroom big enough to use as a study. Cooking and eating and all those other normal things would take place in this house, with Archie and whoever is here at the time. And it would liberate another bedroom for the Lintott brothers, and their families. Or make the little house with an extra bedroom? Just in case,'

She was about to comment on this incredible plan, which seemed to have developed so quickly that it was nearly overwhelming, when Gabriel added, 'But then I had another idea which I think is much better. We could build another wing at right angles on this side, off this bedroom side of the house and have it go along the fence towards the back corner. Long enough to have another bathroom and a couple of bedrooms. But it's all pie in the sky at the moment. Your brothers might not like the idea, and then we'll work out another plan. What do you think about the right angle wing?'

She lay silently considering this and realised that it would be a perfect solution, provided her brothers didn't object, but why would they? Without warning she started to cry, and Gabriel pulled her tight against his chest and kissed her temple. 'I hope you're crying because you're happy, Mopsy.'

28

When Mary woke up again an hour later she was firmly anchored by Gabriel's arm over her midriff with his warm chest behind her back and lay still for several minutes just revelling in the feeling of being so close to him. But soon she had to squirm out from under his arm, and he chuckled behind her. 'I'd just decided I had to let go of you, and now you're awake and I don't need to feel guilty.'

'I have to pee, sorry and then I have to get dressed!' She reached for her T-shirt on the floor and pulled it over her head as she walked to the door. 'There's a separate toilet halfway up the hall, and one in the bathroom next to dad's room if you can't wait.'

Coming out of the bathroom she heard her father doing something in the kitchen at the far end of the long hallway, so she went back to Gabriel's room, located her panties and put them on despite his protests and went to investigate.

'What are you doing, dad? Are you making a cooked breakfast for you or for all of us?'

Archie was standing at the stove and turned with a spatula in his hand. 'Is Gabriel awake? Tell him to get up and come and have some breakfast – it's nearly eight o'clock and you said you've got to be at Mrs Wong's at nine. And you've still got to pack all that stuff from the garage into your car.'

Eight hours later Mary walked back into the kitchen, exhausted and dusty with locks of hair escaping from the topknot she had tied it up in that morning. Gabriel and her dad were at the kitchen bench doing something that involved tomatoes, onion and garlic simmering on the stove, a smell like no other, a harbinger of something delicious. She stood for a moment silently watching and let her eyes rove over what was set out on the table, then she smiled. 'Another pizza dinner, dad? Are you teaching Gabriel how to make them from scratch?'

They both swung around and spoke at the same time. 'You're filthy!' said Archie and Gabriel said, 'You've got dirt on your face.'

'I know, and I'm exhausted. I've been carrying heavy things and lifting dusty sofa cushions - you know those big squab things that form the seat part of the sofa and putting things into boxes and bubble wrap non-stop all day. You wouldn't believe it, but we had put up posters saying that the garage sale, which incidentally took place on the little front lawn, not in the garage, would start at ten and by quarter past nine there were cars lined up for miles and people were milling around looking at all the stuff for sale. Mrs Wong had put up posters in the three supermarkets down that end of town, too, very colourful ones!'

Gabriel studied her smudged face and the corner of his mouth twitched. 'Do you want a shower first or should I pour you a glass of wine right away?'

'Shower – definitely. I'll be back in a couple of minutes.'

Twenty minutes later she returned with her hair wet and slowly pulling up into her usual big lose curls. 'Sorry, I had to wash my hair once I'd had a look in the mirror. It was full of dust and bits of God knows what.' She pointed at Gabriel who was now sitting at the table with a glass of wine in front of him. 'You haven't realised probably, but when you have hair as thick as mine it's a real process washing it and getting it reasonably dry. Not something you do in the last minute unless you want to leave the house with wet hair. If I don't kind of wring it out in a towel and squeeze the water out it drips down my back for the next hour.'

She went to the pantry, picked up the big glass jar of roasted cashew nuts and sat down. 'Wine please! God, I really deserve it today. And that pizza smells good, dad, but why are we having pizza two days running?'

'I told Gabriel yesterday that you'd offered to bring pizza home, but I said I usually make it, a legacy from my Italian mother. And he said he would like to know how to make pizza instead of buying it, so I decided to teach him. But explain the sofa cushions, please.' He sat down at the end of the table and reached for the wine bottle. 'How did they get involved in the garage sale? Was she selling furniture as well?'

Mary laughed at how crazy the day had been. 'It was a total surprise. When I got there, Pat said she was adding some things, and we had to get them out of the house as soon as we finished unloading my car. You know how I spent hours sorting things after I decided to bring all the smaller things over here? So we had several boxes of ornaments and small things, two that said $1 each, two that said $5 each, and then the four boxes with kitchen stuff, and stacks of linen and whatever plus all kinds of electrical gadgets, dozens.'

She drank some of her wine and glanced at the oven and Archie said, 'Don't worry, I've set the timer. We've got another few minutes.'

'OK then. But you know how I spent evenings with Pat after work so we could kind of sort things. Which wasn't possible to do properly because there was nowhere to put things.' She shook her head in amazement at the thought. ' I thought I had a good idea of how much there was, but we probably unearthed at least half as much again. And the stuff behind that sofa we sold! My God, you could stock a shop just with what I found there. Thank God, Doug was there to help!'

'What kind of electrical stuff?' Gabriel looked fascinated. 'I just can't picture it. I've never been inside a hoarder's house.'

'Oh, little vacuum cleaner things, fans, grinders and mixers of all kinds, an ice cream maker and a small coffee maker, most of them never used. In the end we just plonked things straight down on the lawn and made up a price when someone asked what it cost.'

'Sofa squabs,' reminded Gabriel. 'Explain please!'

Giggling now, Mary said, 'She said she'd decided to get rid of some living room furniture since I was there last! One of the two sofas, the huge bulky one, one of the armchairs, two little tables, one lamp and three pictures. As I said, thank goodness for Doug or I'd be broken by now.'

'Remind me who Doug is? You mentioned him before - is that the ex-husband?' Archie raised his eyebrows. 'I thought they weren't talking to each other.'

'No, her ex-husband is called Darren. Doug's the new guy in the flat two doors down – a lovely man, someone else's ex-husband. He's that one who came over the first evening we really got going with the sorting and asked what we were doing, and then he decided to buy some stuff he needed, and when I got there the next night he was already there, directing operations. He's an administrator from the City Council.'

She drank some of her wine and shook her head. 'And *then* at nearly ten, just when the crowd on the front lawn was nearly overwhelming she had me go into Liam's room, because he had been around and got everything he wanted to keep and taken it to his aunt's place, so we dragged out his bed and mattress and a big chest of drawers plus a little study desk and an office type chair – with the help of Doug. She made a fortune!'

She took another sip of wine before she continued. 'Endless carrying things from the piles we had lined up in the hallway, too, more and more stuff on the lawn and Pat negotiating with people because there were no prices on most of those things. Then Maylene turned up and helped, which was great, because it was getting chaotic. Pat and I could never have done it by ourselves. Neither of us had any idea it would turn into such an event.'

Gabriel and Archie had exactly the same expression on their faces now, amusement and slight disbelief, and her father said, 'But how did people pay? Do people bring loads of cash to these things? I've never been to one.'

'Oh, no, but I loaded an app called Stripe on her phone a few days ago, so she could scan cards, and the money went straight into her account, so we wouldn't miss out on a lot of sales. We tried it out with my card and it worked perfectly, so today she was very quick with it.'

She thought for a moment and ran her hands up through her hair to shake out the curls, now drying and taking on their usual appearance. Gabriel watched fascinated and her eyes met his. He's thinking of himself running his hands through my hair, she thought, and smiled. That look! I can't wait to get him into bed!

'And thank God I did that, or we would never have sold so much furniture. All the big pieces went apart from one little side table and the floor rug. People would pay and we put a piece of paper saying "sold" on whatever big thing they'd bought. Some had utility trucks and others went off and returned with a trailer or a truck and took it away – we had four or five people do that.'

And then the timer buzzed and Mary got some plates out for the pizza, and they talked about other things. When Mary was getting ice cream out of the deep freeze Gabriel said behind her, 'So I'll move back to my flat tomorrow and go to work as usual on Monday morning.'

Mary's hands simply stopped, one holding the box of ice cream and the other suspended - she felt as if the world had shifted on its axis. She turned slowly and tried to sound casual. 'Wouldn't it be better to stay here for another couple of days? Until we know for sure you're not going to have a relapse?'

Archie shot her a look full of mischief. 'We haven't told you what we did today while you were out. We tested his health and strength, and this guy is as fit as can be and strong as an ox. Talk about bouncing back, incredible! We drove down to Churchill Park and walked fast around the entire perimeter, a bit too fast for me - about three or four kilometres I would think. And wherever we saw one of those exercise contraptions the City Council put up a few years ago Gabriel used them very energetically. And not a squeak out of his lungs, no breathing problems. I was very impressed. So I think he's safe living on his own.'

Gabriel said as casually as before, 'You're welcome to come and visit, Mopsy. I do want to see you, you know.'

She had to laugh. 'I think our conversation earlier, yours and mine I mean, is playing games with my mind. And the way you two seem to have become such good friends in five minutes made me nearly think you were part of the furniture now, everything's happened so fast.'

Gabriel looked mock-seriously at her. '*Please* don't say

you've changed your mind after chasing me in public to tell me I belong to you! I couldn't bear the humiliation.'

Archie gave a chortle of amusement. 'I don't know what you two want to do, but I'm going to watch the cricket, England versus Australia, but I can do it on my laptop in the old living room if you two want to sit here.'

'What's the old living room?' Gabriel looked intrigued. 'I thought this big space was a living room and a kitchen knocked into one.'

'That part was the dining room.' Archie pointed to the L-shaped space. 'But Marion and I – the boys' mother – decided pretty soon that with lots of kids we wanted a real family space, so we took a wall out and created this. The kitchen was a big old-fashioned kitchen anyway with room for this big table, so we turned it into what is still the centre of family life.'

'And the old living room, where is that?'

Mary smiled. 'I'll give you a tour when we've finished our ice cream and then we can all watch the cricket, or dad can watch it here and we can sit somewhere else.'

They started with the old living room. 'I love this room – I often sit here and read. There's something about it that's so cosy. Those big old French doors with windows both sides, so you nearly feel you're in the garden and the old-fashioned wallpaper. It's the original, would you believe.'

Gabriel studied the room and then looked seriously at Mary, who was watching his eyes move around. 'And you seriously thought there'd be nowhere for us to sit with our friends if they came to visit? Or is this space kept as a sanctum and not used for entertaining?'

'Oh God, no! I sometimes have my little gang of best friends here for drinks and dad has a couple of friends he plays cards with, nearly always in this room. We just use whatever space isn't being occupied by someone else. And when the weather is good we use the deck – a lot. The angle of the kitchen part shelters it a little from the worst winds.'

He chuckled. 'Archie told me about the family cricket games in the garden and how the spectators sit lined up on the deck – it sounds wonderful. While you were at the garage sale he and I had a look around the garden and I could see exactly how a wing along the side would work, plenty of room for what we would need.'

Mary opened the door to the deck and stepped outside and tried to picture that additional wing and what it would look like. 'It would work, provided it's long and not too wide – maybe with a corridor along the neighbour's side and then two bedrooms and a bathroom with windows facing the garden.' She turned to Gabriel who had followed her. 'There would still be plenty of room for the cricket, but we might have to put up a net, like around a tennis court. Just one long stretch or the windows in that wing would be smashed all the time. We're forever sending someone over the fence into Mr Barefoot's garden on that side of us to pick up the ball. He's very tolerant and we give him a bottle of whisky for Christmas every year as a tank you. Isn't it lucky that dad bought this place all those years ago, so we have this huge garden.'

29

They finally went to bed very late after watching the cricket together and Mary wondered who was going to say, "Come and share my bed" - or were they just going to take for granted that she would join Gabriel in his bed where they had spent the previous night? But no decision was necessary. After saying goodnight to her father at the door to his room, Gabriel and Mary continued to the end of the hallway where he stopped by the open door to his room and held it for her and said casually, 'Do you want to use the bathroom first or shall I?'

The implication that they were both going to go into that room, whoever used the bathroom first, made it easy.

'You might want to join me in my room tonight,' said Mary. 'You haven't even seen my room yet.'

'OK, you go in the bathroom first and then I'll come and see you.'

She left her bedroom door open and sat in bed with no

lights on. Gabriel appeared in boxer shorts, closed the door behind him and said, 'Wow, you've got the night sky inside.'

It made her laugh. She had wondered what he would say when he saw her ceiling covered in tiny glowing stars that John had put up a few years ago to replace the originals that had stopped glowing.

'Aren't they nice? What with those and the slight light that comes in through the blind this room is never totally dark, and then when I go out into the passage which I do sometimes at night, there are those night lights plugged into the wall sockets, so it's like a kind of runway of little lights to guide me to the kitchen.'

'Did you always have such a big bed even when you were a little girl?' asked Gabriel and again it made her laugh.

'Oh no, I had a single bed, and I was in this room because with the door open I could see right down the passage from where my bed was placed then, and all the boys would leave their doors open too, so it was like we were all in one big space together. I often got up in the middle of the night and crept into bed with one of them, usually Henry. He was the one who found me, so he was my security blanket.'

'And now you have a queen size bed,' said Gabriel and studied it with a frown. 'No, I think it's a king sized bed. Why do you have such a big bed?'

'I got it two years ago when I got tired of little kids stumbling into my room in the middle of the night and crawling into bed with me, pushing me around and kicking and squirming. When the whole tribe is here these kids just wander around when they wake up in the night - it's like they enjoy having all these people to choose from. And far fewer rules here than when they're at home, I would think.'

Finally Gabriel got in beside her and said, 'I don't have a condom. Do you? Or are you on the pill?'

She was quiet for a moment thinking about the implications of this question and what it might mean. 'I'm not on the pill – never was. Do we need a condom?

He raised himself on one elbow and looked down on her in the dim light. 'I don't know if we need one. What if you get pregnant? Wouldn't you mind?'

Another silence from Mary while she considered this quite seriously, then she said, 'No I don't think I'd mind. Would you?'

'No, not at all – provided it didn't upset your plans to continue to a master's degree.' He chuckled. 'Forty-eight hours in this house, and particularly the time I've spent with Archie, has shown me a side of life I couldn't have imagined before I came here. I would love us to have a child together and raise him or her here, surrounded on occasions by untold uncles and aunts and cousins. And with your dad as a part time babysitter, maybe doing the kindie run? From a few things he said, I think he would like a little body running around the house again.'

She felt tears pooling her eyes. This was not what she had imagined would happen when she organised for Gabriel to come and stay until he got better. She had hoped that they would just build a stronger connection but somehow leaving him alone with her father all day, after they had already had a few hours together on the Friday, had created a level of affection between them that she had not expected. And not only affection but trust too, probably based on the several very personal conversations they seemed to have had.

'He would love it,' she said quietly and put her hand on Gabriel's cheek. 'He would really love it. But just talking about it isn't much point, is it? Not unless we do something a bit more constructive?'

'I can't wait - I've been wanting this for so long. Walking past you with a nod at work, trying to protect you and myself, and aching to reach out and take hold of you. Maybe drag you into the stationery room on the admin floor and ravish you in the dark.'

'I'd love to be ravished by you, anywhere at all.'

The only reply she got was a groan of desire and then it was all on, and she knew that this was for life. Nothing can ever change this relationship, she thought when they lay panting beside each other. I feel as if I'm a character in a romantic novel where a happy ending was always going to happen, where all obstacles are overcome.

She got up to open the window and stood for a moment looking out into the garden where moonlight cast shadows of the trees at the far end. 'A lovely night, in all respects,' she said quietly and went back to sit cross legged just beside Gabriel's shoulder. 'You, my darling,' she said seriously, 'are without a doubt the most deceptive person I have ever met. That was stupendously good! I wasn't expecting that after you told me you hadn't hugged anyone for years. I thought we might have to practise a bit more.'

He laughed quietly and pulled her down and put both arms around her and rocked her a little. 'Ah, but you haven't thought it through, have you? I did have time to develop some skills before what you call the monster face period of my life stopped everything. I'm really glad you enjoyed it. I thought it was marvellous, too - thank you!'

They went to sleep with Mary curled up on her side with her head on Gabriel's shoulder, his around her and his hand warm and strong on her hip. When she woke up because she needed to pee she tried to slide out of bed without waking him up, but he was instantly alert. 'Is something wrong?'

'Oh no, not at all. I just need to go to the toilet.'

When she returned he reached out as soon as she got into the bed and pulled her close again. He kissed her forehead and whispered, 'I love you, Mopsy. I have waited for you forever and now I feels as if my whole life has been leading to this point. This is all I want.'

30

Three days later Mary arrived at work with Gabriel, who had come for dinner the previous evening and stayed the night. When he parked in his usual spot they got out looked at each other over the roof of the car and Mary said seriously, 'It was so lucky you took a shortcut through the row of cars that day and grabbed me, or we probably wouldn't be standing here now. I think I would have been squashed between those cars if you hadn't thrown me to one side. Super-fast reaction, just like that strange man said.'

He shook his head and smiled. 'No, I don't think it would have hit you, not unless you'd moved a fraction in the wrong direction when you heard it coming, but it would have scared you because it would have been very close to where you were standing. I could see the trajectory perfectly – the margin was probably a matter of a few centimetres.'

"Well, whatever,' said Mary and grabbed her bag off the

241

back seat. 'I survived thanks to you and here we are with all our problems sorted. Isn't it lovely?'

Later that morning Mary went to get a cup of coffee and found Gabriel helping himself in the otherwise empty room. 'What are you doing on this floor? I don't often see you here.'

'I've just had a look at Bert's computer. He said he had a problem attaching large files to outgoing emails, but it wasn't really a problem at all. He'd mucked around with the e-mail settings and put a size limit in, so it was easy to fix. God knows why he did it, but it's not the first time. He's a bit random with things like that. Thank goodness he can't get into the back end of the important software.'

He put his mug down on the nearest table, took hers out of her hand and put it beside his own. 'Come here,' he said in that tone of voice that always made her gravitate towards him. He pulled her close and as always when he did this she felt herself relaxing and leaned into him unable to resist getting her whole body as close to him as possible. Then a voice behind them said, 'Wow! What's going on here then?'

They flew apart and found Wendy staring at them looking slightly puzzled, but with a smile hovering somewhere behind the confusion.

'Sorry,' said Mary. 'We're actually engaged, we just haven't t-told anyone yet. And I know we shouldn't b-behave like this at work.'

'Well, keep it turned down if you know what's good for you.' Wendy gave them a sly smile. 'Or you'll have the whole building gossiping about you and taking sneaky photos of you two kissing. Last time we had a company romance going on the whole place became a hive of chatter and speculation.'

They sat down together and spent ten enjoyable minutes talking about work and various things unrelated to themselves, then Gabriel got his feet and left for his office upstairs and Wendy looked at Mary with a little smile. 'How long has this been going on? That day when Gabriel came down to get you logged on to our systems I got no vibe at all that you two had a thing going.'

'We didn't then,' said Mary. 'We had this m-misunderstanding at the very beginning - long b-before that day. But we've sorted it out n-now, so everything's fine.'

'OK, that's good. Congratulations!' said Wendy briskly. 'Now I've got a little problem in Lab 2 that I want you to help me with. Rob's been putting samples through the centrifuge, but he's either clumsy or just slow. I haven't been able to spend enough time watching him to make up my mind why it's so slow, but we need someone whose fingers are a bit more nimble than his are, someone who's really quick, so we can finish putting all those samples through. So what I want you to do is leave that data thing you're doing for me until tomorrow and come into the lab. I'll put you on the centrifuge and move Rob to something else.

A casual rhythm developed over the next week, with Mary spending a couple of nights at Gabriel's flat and he in turn spent more and more time with her and Archie at the house. On the Saturday afternoon Mary left them to watch rugby on TV and went to meet the MAMA gang at the French Bistro. She had suddenly realised that her life had become so full of activity now with her and Gabriel spending so much time together out of work that she hadn't seen her friends for nearly three weeks. She had turned down a date with them last week, but now it was urgent. 'I really must tell them,' she said that day over lunch. 'They're my three best friends.' She turned to Gabriel who was sitting at the kitchen table eating baked beans on toast. 'You've never met them, but I've known them since I was tiny. Andrea used to be my bodyguard walking to and from school, she's a bit older than I am, and the other two are friends of hers, same age as her. One of them Maylene, is the one whose mother had the garage sale a while ago. Anyway I've got to tell them. I couldn't bear it if they found out from someone else. They'd feel so insulted not to have been in my confidence, so I'm meeting them this afternoon. I'll be home at five or half past.'

She turned to Archie and pointed at the fridge. There's a nice piece of lamb in the fridge. I thought we could BBQ it, so if you could put your usual gorgeous spices on it a bit in advance perhaps. It's plenty warm enough now to barbecue and eat on the deck outside.'

Telling the MAMA gang about her suddenly very different life plans turned into a marathon session of questions, excitement and celebration. Mary had thought about where to start and how much she should tell them about the lead-up, so she didn't mention anything apart from saying that Gabriel was a workmate and they had got to know each other at work.

'But how did this happen so fast?' asked Andrea looking thoroughly confused. 'One minute you haven't had a boyfriend of any kind for three years and now suddenly you don't just have a boyfriend, you're going to get married. And we've never heard of this guy.'

'And not only that.' said Maylene. 'The worst thing is that we've never met him, and he's not been vetted and okayed by us. She's just made-up her mind without even consulting us! It's outrageous, girls.'

Ava looked around the table, studied each face, paused briefly on Mary and said decisively in her police officer voice, 'I know how to find out all about him. I'll arrest him, I'll say I saw him push a woman deliberately out of the way or something, so I can arrest him for assault and then I'll be able to question him. Sit him down in an interview room, handcuff him to the table and shine strong lights straight into his face and grill him for hours on end.'

Mary just smiled. She had known that this conversation would turn into total chaos, and she was thoroughly enjoying the surprise she had sprung on them. 'Calm d-down, girls,' she said now. 'Just stop and listen, will you? This is *not* a n-new and sudden thing, and I'm not b-being impulsive or getting carried away by sexual attraction and llust. Not that there isn't sexual attraction between us, b-but that's not why I'm going to get married to him. I've known him for months, ever since he rescued me when I was l-locked into the dark stationary room and couldn't get out, and there was n-no light switch, and no door handle on the inside either. And you know what happens to m-me in dark spaces with no light.'

'So, you knocked on the door, and he came past and let you out? Is that all it was?' Andrea looked as if she felt this sounded suspiciously like an excuse, a made-up story. 'And then you fell in love with him on the spot?'

'Oh God, no, he was in there too, though I didn't know that b-because it's quite a long room where they keep all kinds of supplies, n-not just stationery. And it's got all these freestanding shelf units that k-kind of divides it up into bays - he was at the f-far end from where I was, and someone closed the d-door and suddenly it went d-dark. Turns out he thought there was a p-puppy in there, but it was me moaning quietly, totally taken over by that p-panic thing that overwhelms me when I'm alone in the dark. And he f-found me, just grabbed hold of me and held me for about fifteen m-minutes.'

She ended up having to tell them the whole story, all the details, step by step. How she didn't know what he looked like, but she knew what his skin smelled like. How she stood behind him really close in the lift when those awful guys we're talking about her, and she realised that it was the man from the stationary room right there in front of her. She told them about the ensuing conversation when they got out of the lift, how he gave her the stone coin and how she told him that he belonged to her, and they all laughed. Ava said on a note of disbelief, 'You told a perfect stranger that he belonged to you? Are you crazy?'

"But he gave me his m-magic stone coin,' said Mary reasonably, as if that explained everything. 'And then I hijacked him in a cafe once and m-made him go for a walk with me. And I could tell that he l-loved me, I could feel it. It was such a strong f-feeling - like a swirl of warm air around me. I knew his hands were just twitching to t-take hold of me and hug me.'

'You still haven't explained why this was such a torturous process,' complained Maylene frowning as she tried to make sense of the story. 'If he was that attracted to you, why didn't he act on it. I mean you had told him that you loved him. So what was the problem? Don't tell me is married!'

'Oh, for God's sake,' said Mary. 'D-don't be so silly. I couldn't very well m-marry him if he's already married, could I? No, it was his scar. He's g-got a huge lumpy scar down one side of his f-face.'

This revelation necessitated another whole raft of explanations, and then they got to the Lintott line-up, which they had all seen on social media. 'Aha!' exclaimed Ava.' So *he* was the guy who alerted your brothers, and he filmed it. Brilliant.'

Once they got over the surprise and started feeling excited instead of simply curious or worried, Maylene suddenly remembered that the others would know nothing about what Mary had done for her mother, and though she had decided from the start that she would never tell anyone apart from Mary about her mother's chaotic flat, she now decided they needed to know.

'Confession time! Listen to this!' she said. 'You guys think that this girl is just a cute thing with curly hair, who's also very smart of course, and now she's suddenly hooked up with this – whatever he is. Maybe he's a hunk? Well never mind, we'll find out eventually. She also sorted out a family problem relating to my mom. You just wait till I tell you.'

When the story was told, Mary pulled her phone out. 'This is the text m-message Maylene sent me after she went to visit her m-mother, when we had nearly t-totally tidied up her flat and got the garage sale sorted out.' She read out the message that started with four exclamation points followed by "what have you done with my mother".

'Right!' Andrea got to her feet. 'We definitely need another drink – my round. This is completely amazing - I don't think I've heard so many surprising things in one go in my whole life. I hope nobody's driving because whoever is driving can't have another drink.'

Once back at the house, Mary heard the men talking as soon as she opened the front door, her father's lighter voice and Gabriel's much deeper tones. They seemed to be debating something with great energy, but when she heard her father say, 'Yes, and I think the idea of the corridor that someone had, was it James? That wasn't so good.' she stopped to listen. What on earth were they talking about?

'I know,' said Gabriel, 'but I still think that Henry and Richard, and you and I are on the right track - we all agree with Mary's idea that the corridor should be at the back because that way all the bedrooms and the bathroom will look out over the garden, which is really nice. And do we really care that we have to put up a cricket type screen just stop all the windows being smashed all the time?

'Yeah, it is a good idea,' said Archie. 'But I also think that William's idea that we put shutters on the windows is something that will fit the whole look of the place. Better than having that kind of wire netting screen. Whenever a cricket match is about to start we just shut the shutters and there's no glass for the balls to smash - because there are bound to be balls in that direction, there always are.'

Mary walked into the kitchen and found the men preparing dinner and so engrossed in their discussion that they didn't even hear her coming in.

'Hi guys, are you talking about the proposed bedroom wing? It sounds as if you've already discussed it with the boys.'

'Yeah, we did,' said Gabriel. 'Archie thought it was a good idea seeing the cricket on TV was rained out and it was a day when they might all be at home, so we talked to them on Teams. Sorry to leave you out of it, but I think I represented you quite well. I remembered all your points, and we had a really good discussion.'

Archie turned from cutting potatoes into wedges. 'We're going to get a good architect to come in and measure things up and draw the plans, but I think everyone agreed that another two bedrooms, quite big, and a bathroom between them would be perfect. Your idea of having the corridor at the back closest to the neighbour's fence was voted for and won by a majority.'

'Well that was quick!' Mary grinned. 'I thought this will take forever to organise. And what about the various aspects of who owns it – now or later?'

'No, problem – it' sorted. William says he knows how to set it up so there are not problems in the future and until then Archie owns the house, I pay for the extra wing, and everyone is happy. No need to be complicated.'

'And this surprised me,' said Archie. 'Yolanta is pregnant! They're getting married just quietly before Christmas. Her father is having cancer treatment, so they don't want a big wedding, and they want to have it soon. So there's another little body to run around the house creating havoc. Williams suggested we turn one bedroom into a bunk room with three sets of bunks for the kids to move into as they get old enough – well, some of them are old enough already. So that takes care of six, maybe eight and all the adults will have a quiet night perhaps.'

They had barbecued lamb steaks covered in herbs and crushed garlic with roasted potato wedges and a tomato salad sitting on the deck in the warm evening. They continued discussing the bedroom wing as it was now called and agreed that with a garden as large as this one there was no need to worry about using up a bit of space.

'I just thought of another thing - just this moment. You know how that westerly wind from the mountains can be so chilly even way into spring? Well, the bedroom wing will create a nice angle and shelter the deck.'

That night in bed Gabriel told her more about the discussion he and Archie had with her brothers. 'I think he'd already talked to them as a group – about us living here,' he said. 'They were all very positive about the idea and it felt as if they'd had a thorough discussion about it earlier. Everyone thinks it would be good for Archie, but not only that. It also means we're able to look after him if he needs it as he gets older, so a win-win situation. Not that they said that outright, it just filtered through gradually from various comments. And as Henry said right at the end, just before you returned, it means a lot to them that this remains the central place for the family as a whole. This tribe mentality you lot have is so valuable and so precious – not just for all you siblings but for the future of those children too.'

Much later when Mary was dropping off to sleep a thought popped into hr head out of nowhere and she wondered if maybe she and Gabriel should get married before Christmas too, because what was the point of waiting. She could tell that Gabriel was already asleep and decided to mention it in the morning, fell asleep and had a vivid dream of watching a little boy with curly black hair and a puppy running up the hallway from her bedroom to the kitchen.

31

By the time the Christmas holiday break arrived, the Lintott household which now permanently included Gabriel, had been unusually busy, and some of the arrangements that had been made were new and not without problems.

They had worked hard and fast to get things into place, and tonight they had cleared the final hurdle. Christmas Day fell on a Monday this year, so the actual festive period would become an extension of the weekend, and then the same would apply the following weekend with New Year's Day on a Monday.

'What a great thing it is we have these statutory days off after Christmas and New Year,' said Gabriel one evening after two sessions on the Teams app, one of which had lasted an hour and a half, complicated and intricate, but it had ended on a positive note. 'It's going to make it such a lovely long break now that Tidewell's have decided to give us those in-between days off.'

'I still think it's a pity not to wait with the wedding, you know.' Archie looked seriously at Mary, who was curled up in the corner of the sofa, half lying down with a cushion under her head. 'I'm sure Gabriel's parents would love to be present whatever they just said, and they'll be here in July for the baby. He is their only son after all.'

'I think they're genuinely OK with it.' Gabriel looked thoughtfully at Mary, who was looking a bit better than she had since late afternoon. 'Seeing how sick Mary feels both in the mornings and in the evenings, we have to respect her wishes. And we both want to be married before the baby arrives. And as my dad just said, we can livestream a private little wedding ceremony, so they can feel that they're present.'

Mary lifted ahead from her cushion and set up straight, sat absolutely still for a few moments and smiled. 'I think it's over for tonight, thank God. I never realised that feeling nauseated could practically ruin your life. My doctor says I'm very unusual possibly unique, to have this six hour period in the middle of the day when I'm perfectly well and can eat, and then the nausea returns late afternoon.'

'But we knew that already,' said Gabriel and patted her hand. 'I mean that you are unique. I don't think anyone in the family would question that.'

Archie picked up Mary's glass of water. 'Would you like some lemonade now or some ginger ale? You must be hungry too – or is it too soon? I'll heat up your helping now if you like.'

'Thanks, I'd love some food, I'm starving now. And

lemonade first please, with ice if we have any.' She got up and stretched. 'And I do think that Teams meeting with the boys ended really well, don't you? What a bonus that app is - to be able to load the architect's plans on it so we could all see exactly what we were talking about at the same time, that was good. And the sketch of the front of the new wing with shutters on all the windows and the roofline exactly the same as on the house - everyone liked it as much as we do.'

'Now all we have to do is find a builder and get the consent organised.' Archie returned from the kitchen end of the room and put a glass of lemonade beside Mary. 'Your dinner will be warm in ten minutes. I know a couple of chaps who have sons, who are builders. One of them is the guy James did his apprenticeship with, but if James would like to do it, as he said, he'll have to get leave from his current job.'

'Let's hope he can. It would be nice to have him working here, but I don't know what Yolanta would think about it. With a baby on the way she might want him at home. I know they only live a couple of hours away, but it's not as if he would commute every day, is it?'

'We'll just have to wait and see,' said Gabriel in his practical way. 'And even if James could take it on, he'd have to find another couple of guys to work with him, so he doesn't have to do everything on his own. But we have time - getting the building consent from the council will take ages, it always does these days. I think getting those plans drawn up and then readjusted and readjusted and now finally approved by everyone, that's the biggest hurdle out of the way. It's not as if there's a shortage of opinions in this family, is there?'

The three of them looked at each other and Archie said, 'I brought them all up the question everything and this is the result. Seven different opinions every time something comes up, if you include me in the count.'

'Apart from if it relates to Mary's happiness or safety. Then you're all on the same track, entire and instant agreement. So, are we going to get married at Christmas when they're all here, or before Christmas?'

Mary turned a shocked face in his direction and said in a voice of utter disbelief, 'You can't be serious! I'd never get married without the boys around me. The other day when we were talking on the phone John asked who was going to give me away, and I said you're *all* going to give me away, dad and you lot. He laughed, but he said he also had tears in his eyes.'

Gabriel gave her a sly grin. 'I was only kidding, Mopsy - of course we'd never get married without them here.'

'OK,' said Archie when he put Mary's food in front of her after filling his and Gabriel's glasses of wine. 'Now we're past that opinionated discussion about the new wing and all the rest of it, and we've talked to your parents, and it all seemed to be fine - now we need to get down to the detailed plans, because there's a lot to think of and we've got to get it right. We haven't got a lot of time.'

'Oh, I've already been thinking about it,' said Mary around a mouthful of pasta carbonara. 'You know, just in the back of my head while I've been doing other things. I think we have the wedding on the Saturday provided they can all arrive on the Friday. If they can't arrive on the Friday, then we have it on the Sunday, which is Christmas Eve. And I would like to be married in the garden here at home like we talked about the other day, under the plum tree perhaps. And very few guests, just the MAMA girls from my side.' She pointed her fork at Gabriel. 'I don't think I told you, but your cousin will come, because they're not going away for Christmas this year. I talked to Bonita the other day when I met her in the supermarket. She said they're going to be around, and they'd love to come whichever day it is. They'll make sure that they're not booked up, and even if they are they'll cancel whatever it was.'

She smiled. 'I'll tell you what she actually said word for word. She said, she couldn't believe that Gabriel's actually getting married, she'd resigned herself to thinking that he was going to be single all his life for some reason she had never understood, and she told me she'd tried to hook him up with various women, but nothing had worked. And as she said, what a waste it would be for such a wonderful man not to be married and have a family.'

'You're going to make me cry any minute now,' said Gabriel. 'That's very touching, I didn't realise that she thought of me as much as that.'

Archie got up from his chair and groaned. 'OK, guys, I think I need to go to bed. I've had a long day and measuring up where the new wing will be and putting pegs in the ground for the boys to see has done my back in. Let's set aside time tomorrow to do some further planning about the actual wedding, we've only got three weeks now.'

By the time the weekend of the wedding dawned, everything Mary could possibly think of had been planned, shopped for and tucked away in the fridge and the pantry which was bulging with supplies. The tribe had arrived in dribs and drabs through from Friday afternoon to midday on the Saturday and they had all been shocked by how nauseated and ill Mary was for several hours on Friday afternoon and again on the Saturday morning.

When John went to see how she was feeling that morning he found her leaning against the wall in the hallway just outside her bedroom, pale faced and exhausted looking. 'Oh, Mopsy!' he exclaimed and pulled her into a gentle hug. 'You poor little thing – I had no idea it was this bad. Where are you going?'

She leaned into him and rested her head against his chest. 'I've just been sick again and then cleaned my teeth, which is all I have the energy to do. I want to go and sit on the sofa in the kitchen, so I can be where everyone else is. Or on the deck perhaps.'

'Shouldn't you be lying down?' He rocked slowly back and forth, holding her steady. 'You look too sick to walk.'

She chuckled quietly. 'You won't believe the change that happens suddenly about ten when this lets up. It's like being reborn – suddenly I feel fine but starving, and then I'm OK until half past three or so.' She lifted her head and looked up at his concerned face. 'Which is why the wedding tomorrow is at one o'clock – gives me a good safety margin.'

They walked down the hallway with John's arm around her, and she sat on the deck in the shade, watching everyone milling around, checking the pegs that marked where the bedroom wing would be, and repeatedly circling back to her chair to make sure she didn't need anything.

'I knew it would be like this,' she said quietly to Gabriel, who returned from a late shopping trip just after the daily miracle of the nausea lifting. 'I had to marshal all my patience and put up with the concern and the offers of help, but I'm glad to be back on my feet now. It's quite tiring being an invalid. Did you get the bubble blower?'

'It's in the car. I'll get it out tomorrow just before the ceremony. I wonder where Archie got the idea from, quite an odd thing for him to suggest.'

'It was that birthday celebration he went to at a friend's place last year – a party for a nine-year old grandchild, I think. He said it was lovely seeing kids running around trying to catch the big bubbles. He must have stored the idea up ever since.'

Mary and Gabriel were married in the garden on Christmas Eve, with only a handful of non-family present. A buffet lunch was delivered from Westmoreland's and set out in the kitchen and Mary lasted through hugs and kisses, congratulations and questions about how she was feeling until half past four when nausea struck again. Hoping not to soil her gorgeous white linen dress she rushed to the bathroom, was violently sick and retired to her bedroom after putting the sign Gabriel had written on the outside of her door: "Please do not disturb – I will reappear about eight or so, starving."

Christmas Day followed the same pattern, but the afternoon interval of normal life again lasted an hour longer, which made it seem possible that this tiresome time might be waning. When Mary came back to normal again earlier than she had for weeks and appeared on the deck everyone cheered.

'Most of us have had dinner,' said Archie, 'and all the kids have eaten, but there's plenty of the buffet left.' So she sat with the others on the deck with a plate on a little table beside her and watched a noisy game of cricket, relaxed and happier than ever.

'It's interesting that you've suddenly got a little better,' said Yolanta, who had never had a day of morning or evening sickness during her pregnancy. 'So today the total hours were two less than yesterday, that's very promising!'

Sylvia, who was on Mary's other side, leaned across. 'I was sick only in the very early mornings and it didn't last long, but my God! What you're going through is just terrible, so I hope it stops soon.'

'I think it m-might, you know. The whole n-nausea thing was less intense today. But I'm g-going to make damn sure we take precautions when this one's b-born and we have a normal married life again – I think I conceived the f-first time we had sex!'

Their screams of laughter alerted everyone, and her comment was repeated by Sylvia who thought it was hilarious. 'Listen to this!' she said. 'These two move fast, very fast.'

'After a slow start and lots of misunderstandings.' Gabriel seemed unfazed by the hilarity and Mary shook her head at some of the comments that followed.

At dusk they started up the bubble machine again and sat on the deck watching the children race around. 'A perfect day,' said Mary. 'A perfect weekend!'

EPILOGUE
FIVE YEARS LATER

For once Gabriel got home earlier than Mary, who had a doctor's appointment at the ante-natal clinic after work. Archie was in the kitchen where Leonardo, aged four, was building a Lego tower and talking to himself while he worked as he always did; an endless stream of comments on his own progress and instructions to himself about what to do next.

'He's like a funny, little old man,' Archie had said recently when they were all in the kitchen and Leo was chatting away to himself. 'And I don't mean an old man like me, I'm an exception, of course. But I had an old uncle on my mother's side, who was just like that. He was constantly telling himself what he should do next and commenting on how he was getting on - very amusing.'

Gabriel kicked his damp shoes off inside the front door and came into the kitchen with his bag and a paper parcel in his hands.

'Lego hazard today, so watch your step seeing you're in your socks,' said Archie, who was sitting at the table doing the crossword in the daily paper. 'There are probably bits of the stuff everywhere. The nanny left a bit earlier than usual and she hadn't had time to tidy up the Lego bits, so they're still all over the floor. She had to rush off to deal with something she called a minor emergency with a parental unit – I gather that's what she calls her parents. I'll do the Lego sweeping later, Leo's still got a way to go with that tower.'

Gabriel dropped his bag in the corner by the door, put the parcel on the kitchen bench and sat down opposite Archie. 'How was your day? Wasn't it today you were starting that veteran golf tournament?'

'Day one today, then we continue tomorrow and the next day, and then we'll see. I think we have a pretty good chance this year. Since Brendan had to stop playing, our team is a lot stronger than it used to be. The new guy we added as a fourth is very good - nearly as good as I am.'

'Well that's saying something.' Gabriel grinned. 'The way you beat me every time is incredible. Not that I'm very good, but I'm more than forty years younger than you are, so I should be able to put up a good fight.'

They looked at each other and grinned at this constant refrain at the end of every conversation about golf.

Suddenly Leo looked up and said calmly, 'Oh, Daddy's home.' and Archie shook his head. 'Isn't it amazing how he doesn't notice when one of us comes in? You'd think he would have seen you straight away and leapt on you, but it's the same when Mary comes home or me for that matter. He doesn't pay attention till a few minutes later.'

'Well of course he doesn't.' Gabriel looked at his son, who was once again absorbed in his building project and paying no attention. 'He's so secure he hardly notices when we come and go. What with having had the same nanny ever since he was six months old and you at home at least half the time it's like he's got more than just the usual two parents. No need to develop separation anxiety. It's like that old saying that a child should be brought up by a village, but we're doing it on a smaller scale.'

Just then the front door opened, and they both looked up, though it had to be Mary, of course. Leo paid no attention, which surprised nobody.

'What did the doctor say?' asked Archie. 'Did they give you a due date?'

'Third week in March or thereabouts, and it's not twins, thank goodness. I don't think Justine would stay with us if I produced two babies in one go.'

They started dinner preparations and in the practiced routine that had developed between the three of them over the last few years they got things done without tripping over each other. Gabriel set the table before he took Leo away to wash his hands, Mary made dinner and Archie did a stock take in the pantry and the fridge and wrote a shopping list for himself for the next day.

'You're so sexy when you're pregnant,' whispered Gabriel and pulled Mary into a hug when Archie's back was turned, and she laughed quietly. 'Take that X-rated look off your face before you burn the house down! And if you say it in front of Leo you'll have to be the one who explains what it means.'

Behind them Archie chuckled. 'We had a little chat about the flowers and the bees as they used to say – yesterday over lunch, brought on by his question about where the new baby is going to come from.' He grinned. 'He thinks you're trying to fool him by saying it's growing inside his mother. I didn't go into any details and kept it very basic, but neither did I resort to lies about finding babies in the cabbage patch. Any day now he's going to ask for more information. He's *so* like his mother, never content with half an explanation.'

After dinner Archie poured Gabriel and himself another glass of wine and said, 'Right, now I've got a surprise for you. Next weekend, when everyone's here for my eightieth birthday, we're going to have a very special family photo taken, the whole tribe and this time including me. This new guy I play golf with - his son is a professional photographer. and he came over here yesterday afternoon, and we had a look around, so we could pick a really good place for the photo. I've been thinking about this for a while, and I want it to be taken with something in the background that's significant.'

'What a nice idea! We've never had a family photo with you in it. I don't know why we never thought of it, how weird.' Mary frowned as she thought about this. 'And what did you decide on? I mean for a place for the photo?'

'At first I thought we'd do it in the old living room like with all the Christmas photos, but Phil suggested that we line up in front of the house, and he'll take it at an angle. He'll stand a bit out from the corner of the garage, so you can see the enormous oak behind the people on the left. And I think it might look good. It means half of the front of the house will show behind us, and some can stand on the front steps, which means that it won't just be one long row.'

'Let's go outside and have a look.' Gabriel got up. 'Did he really think he'd be able to include the oak as a background?'

They spent a few minutes standing at the garage corner and concluded that the photographer was right. It would probably work, and having people on the three steps up to the front door would work well. 'Not to mention that even with people standing on the steps the fanlight over the front door will show, such a nice feature.' Gabriel pointed at the semi-circular leadlight window that Mary had taken for granted all her life and never thought of as important. 'You're right, it will look lovely.'

'Or maybe,' said Mary after thinking for a few moments, 'we could have all the kids sitting and standing on the steps like in a group all together, some higher than the others.'

Once inside again, Mary turned to Gabriel. 'You never told me if your parents are going to be back this Christmas. It's two years since last time they came, and there's no way I'm going to travel to the other side of the world with Leo and while I'm pregnant. Actually, I can't imagine ever not being here for Christmas. I'm sorry, I'm being greedy about how important these things are in this family.'

'They're important to me too, now that I'm part of the tribe, so nothing to worry about. But listen, I haven't had time to tell you yet, I got a reply from dad this morning and I got a real surprise. Mum and dad are moving back here in February. He said they decided suddenly that they've lived abroad for long enough, and they want to be back here, so their grandchildren don't grow up without knowing them properly. Dad's handed in his notice as of the end of January and mum's leaving her job before Christmas. They've got their eye on a place in one of the western suburbs, halfway up the hills, so we'll have to go and inspect it and report back to them. Maybe take a few photos and check out whatever they ask us to have a good look at.'

The eightieth birthday celebration turned into the kind of semi organised chaos it always did now. With ten children and fourteen adults the preparations had changed a little. The shopping was done as usual one evening with Mary and Archie repeating their well-rehearsed routine with two trolleys and checking out separately. All the beds were now made by the three of them working as a team; the row of bedrooms in the original part of the house and the two bedrooms in the new wing tackled from one end to the other. The discussion about whether to let people make their own beds had stalled before the last family event, but as Mary had said, they could revisit it at any time, it was just that she had always made all the beds in advance and it was a quick and easy thing to do now they did it together. The bunk room had solved a lot of problems and Leo was delighted to be in amongst the other children when they all gathered.

'Eight kids in one room, they'll never go to sleep,' said William when he realised the scale of the bunkroom. But it worked after a fashion with some falling asleep from exhaustion despite others talking and laughing, and eventually total silence.

The family photo turned into utter chaos with so many suggestions about how to arrange it that Gabriel took charge - the first time he had asserted any authority when they were all together. After half an hour of debate, changes of mind, new suggestions and soon nobody really listening to anyone else, Gabriel pulled a piece of paper out of his pocket and said loudly, 'OK, everyone – could you please listen to me for a minute? I had a feeling this might happen, so I did some advance planning. Let's try this and see if it works. Everyone over here please, and then line up from right to left, the way I say.'

A couple of minutes later they were nicely arranged, three brothers with their partners to the right of the steps, all the kids on the three steps and the rest to the left with some shorter women in front of the taller men. The photographer moved three steps further back with his tripod to get them all in the frame and it was done.

'Very masterful,' whispered Mary as she leaned into Gabriel in their bedroom a few minutes later. 'There are so many opinionated people in this tribe now, so someone needs to take charge. Hold me tight, please.'

And as always when she asked to be held tight, he pulled her closer and slid one hand up through her hair to hold her firmly against his shoulder and she sighed. 'Oh God, how I love to be held by you!'

When they walked into Westmoreland's that evening, Mary noticed that yet again at least one person was filming them and knew the video would appear on social media nearly straight away. The restaurant manager had called her after John's fortieth earlier in the year and said that they had tried to talk to diners about not doing this and she had just laughed.

'Don't worry about it. As a tribe we're so used to it now, the internet is full of clips of either the Lintott line-up, as they call it, or just us coming and going from Westmoreland's - it doesn't matter. But thanks for trying!'

And for the first time, when she stood to make her announcement once they were seated in the larger of the two private dining rooms, she looked into Gabriel's eyes instead of Henry's and didn't stammer when she told them that the dessert this time was going to be a surprise, and the lights would be turned off before it was carried in. 'So keep track of the toddlers,' she warned. 'We don't want any kids being trampled on.'

Amazing, she thought and sat down, I still stammer with my sisters-in-law and their children, so weird.

At the end of the evening she looked around the room and mentally added two more babies before next year's tribal gatherings and thought how fortunate it was that they still mostly managed to have the entire tribe coming together for at least two events each year. She smiled at Henry, who was watching her thinking and said, 'Isn't this perfect?'

THANK YOU

We hope you've enjoyed reading this story and would consider leaving a review, or even a rating.

These are not only much appreciated, they also help other readers discover new authors.

For other titles from Lightpool Publishing, please read on.

ABOUT SASKIA

Saskia Woodhill is an author of soft romance novels where slightly paranormal characters occasionally engage in outrageous behaviour and sometimes find themselves in funny or dangerous situations - or funny and dangerous at the same time. Stories that will make you laugh and cry and turn the pages to a satisfying ending.

ALSO FROM SASKIA

Alba's abrupt exit in the middle of an interview for a dream job sets off a chain of events she never saw coming. The inexplicable dread she occasionally feels isn't her imagination, it's a warning signal, one that others don't sense. But this time simply walking away wasn't enough - now a powerful man is determined to discover why she left.

Follow Alba on her intense, emotional journey of secrets, risk-taking and life-changing decisions into a world where the stakes are high, trust is precious, and her future hangs in the balance. This story will keep you riveted, questioning fate and the power of love.

Available from all good bookshops.

Julia, owner of a successful garage and used to working with men, prides herself on her practical and down-to-earth nature. But her calm and orderly world is about to change forever.

After a concussion, she disturbingly starts hearing the thoughts of others as spoken words in her mind. First, it's her sister, then it's Milton, the sexy customer with the sarcastic smile, and the man Julia is irresistibly drawn to, despite his outrageous thoughts.

Available from all good bookshops

A timeslip story with a difference: a lonely widow, a man who came from nowhere, and a sensual, slow-burn romance.

When a naked stranger collapses through Abigail's front door on a snowy night, her usual caution deserts her. Instead of calling the police, she finds herself harbouring this mysterious man who claims to be from the future.

But not her future – a future in another dimension.

Despite her scepticism of anything paranormal—and her hard-learned wariness of men interested in her wealth—something about him breaks through all her defences.

Available from all good bookshops.

To Amy some men had a scent signature, an aroma that preceded them as they got close. Fried onion, lemon grass or cloves, pleasant smells. It was a signal that a particular man had the potential to become a close friend or lover, and the same scent would always accompany him as he approached her.

There had only been one misfire and that was Simon, and she could never understand why she had not realized that his signature smell of overheated cooking oil meant trouble?

Meeting two men with appealing scent signatures nearly at the same time, freshly made coffee for one and cinnamon for the other, seemed nearly too good to be true. But Amy's life became complicated when the man she fell in love with turned out to have a hidden side.

Her plan to teach him a lesson turned into a recipe for disaster and heartbreak, and she was forced to realize that the scent signature might not always be as accurate as she had thought. But a blizzard, a train stuck in the middle of nowhere and the intervention of fate all played a part in the outcome.

OTHER TITLES FROM
LIGHTPOOL PUBLISHING

Letters from the Past by Tina Clough is a series of stand-alone novels where a letter from or about the past reveals something that changes a woman's perceptions of her family, and affects her outlook on life. Life can change in a moment and sometimes you have to step into the unknown and take a chance on love.

Having had nobody in her life since her husband died, Lara unexpectedly finds herself involved with three men. One is planning to use her, one she plans to use for her own ends, and one becomes a "friend-with-benefits" with surprising results. Sometimes a quiet schoolteacher is not all she seems at first glance.

Callista experiences an event of apparent ESP at the Okehampton Castle ruins and becomes a media sensation, but the effect it has on her life is dramatic. How do two people, one calm. one seriously claustrophobic, who feel they are poles apart, cope for an hour and a half in total darkness in a stalled lift? And can they handle the consequences?

Sofia's life is in turmoil: a difficult diva mother, a letter with a confession about a family killing and having to accept help from a man she loathes when she is injured. Can reluctant attraction turn into love?

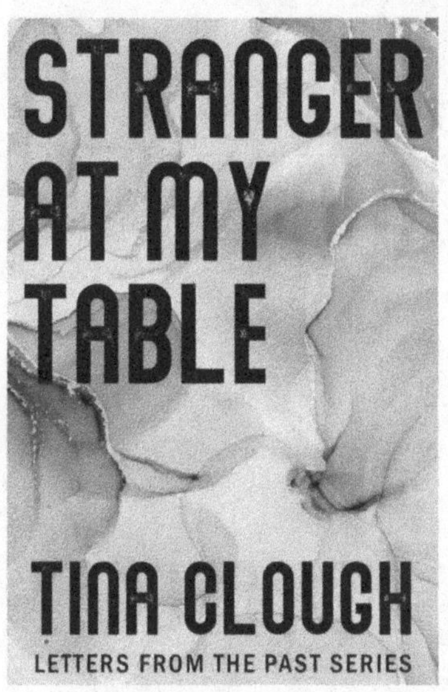

Who is the stranger living in the empty house Miranda inherited from her grandmother? Why is he living like a secretive recluse in someone else's house? Reckless Miranda decides to confront him, and what she discovers prompts her to set out on a fearless quest to bring justice to a man who has given up hope. But is the gamble too great or a risk worth taking?

When Emma finds an old letter in a library book she is instantly intrigued, but by researching the origin of the letter she unwittingly opens the door to danger and becomes the target for threats and harassment. Nearly desperate, she takes a leap of blind faith into the unknown and accepts an offer of help from a stranger - but can she trust him?

Jamie, an ardent protester against the gigantic Vista Resort development and Leo Masters, the high-powered developer, seem unlikely to ever agree on anything. But unexpected coincidences and chance brings them together in a fragile state of mutual respect. Will courage and kindness resolve the situation, or do they need help?

After a bizarre accident with ESP overtones, the media haunt Arapera. But can she trust an offer of help from a man she has only met once? Or will she regret it for the rest of her life if she doesn't take the chance? Sometimes life is a knife-edge balance between staying safe and taking risks, and there is no way of predicting if the gamble is worth it.

When crime-writer Saskia finds an unconscious stranger, she has a strange and strong emotional connection. Pretending to be his cousin and with no thought for the consequences, she spends weeks at his hospital bedside. But what will happen when he wakes and discovers she has invaded his life, breached his privacy and made crucial decisions on his behalf?

THE GIRL WHO LIVED TWICE

What would you do if you woke up one morning and found that time had rewound exactly a year? Would you revisit your past mistakes and try to do better? Would you try to get revenge on those who had wronged you? Or would you use what you knew to get rich? When Mia finds herself in her own past, she must decide how best to use her pre-knowledge of one year's worth of events and personal issues.

9 781738 622030